# WOLF OF STARLIGHT

BOOK 6 OF THE SHIFTER REJECTED SERIES.

AMELIA SHAW

# CHAPTER 1
# GALEN

"Fuck." My throat was raw, but that didn't stop the agony of losing Talia from wrenching another howl of pain from me.

My mate was gone. Taken right out from under my nose. Literally. I should have seen this coming. *How had I not seen this coming?* I'd brought Darius into the Long Claw pack and assigned him roles and responsibilities that I wouldn't have under normal circumstances.

But things were about as far from normal as you could get.

Demons plagued our town, witches had taken up camp on Long Claw land and my pack was at war with the Northwood pack. I was in Alaska with Talia, chasing after a demon wolf pack, along with the truth about her family, and their wolves' red eyes.

We'd found them, and a hell of a lot more than we bargained for.

It had been one emergency after another since I met Talia

and Alaska was no exception. Captured, caged and beaten to near death, Talia's clansmen did their best to tear us apart. They crowned her Princess of the Bone Clan and planned to offer her to their demon wolf god, forcing her to marry and mate with him.

Except Darius beat them to it. They didn't see him coming, either.

Fate was not without a sense of irony. I'd brought Talia into my pack to keep her at my side and keep her safe. Instead, my pack ended up being her undoing. I lost her to another member of my pack—a traitor in our midst.

It was a royal clusterfuck.

Every decision I'd made as Alpha, before and after my father's death, could and should be called into question. My short reign had been an unmitigated disaster. From the moment I concocted that stupid plan to kidnap Talia and use her as a bargaining chip against the Northwood pack, I'd put my own people at risk.

And I'd do it again.

If I hadn't, I might never have found my mate. Cast out and on the run with Darius and a legion of demons haunting her every step, Talia wouldn't have survived on her own. Not that she fared much better at my side.

Still, I wouldn't change a thing, not if it cost me one second with her.

I never expected to fall in love with her, but the moment my wolf and I laid eyes on Talia, I was a goner. I had to find her. Mating mark or not, she was the other half of my heart, my soul, and I would never be complete without her.

But I had to escape the Deofol pack first.

Glass crunched underfoot as I padded barefoot out of the bathroom, leaving a path of bloody prints on the carpet in my wake. I'd destroyed it in a fit of blind rage when Darius pulled Talia into the shadows and disappeared. Bits of broken mirror, drywall and tile littered the floor and a geyser of water spewed from busted faucets.

It didn't get me any closer to finding Talia, but at least my mind was clear, and I could think. Because I needed a plan.

"Princess?" Valerie's thin voice wavered on the other side of the bedroom door. "Talia, is everything all right? I heard raised voices and sounds of a struggle. Open the door, please."

The high-ranking wolf from the Bone Clan knocked on the door. Each rap of her knuckles on the wood came closer and closer together until they blurred into one continuous sound.

"She's gone." I ripped open the door, yanked the wide-eyed demon wolf inside Talia's bedroom and shut it behind her. "And you're going to help me find her."

"What? What do you mean, she's gone?" The blood drained from Valerie's face as she broke free of my grip on her wrist. "How is that possible?"

"It seems your god got tired of waiting." I moved about the room in search of anything I could use to escape the encampment and survive the frozen hellscape outside. "He sent Darius to come and get her."

"Darius? Who the hell is that?" She crossed her arms over her chest and narrowed her gaze. "If she's really gone, why are you still here? This could just be a clever ruse so the two of you can run off together. It won't work. You should just accept the role of consort, the role you agreed to with Galen. It would be so much easier. Gods are fickle and bore easily. He won't occupy all her time."

"I told you, she's gone. So, spare me the sales pitch, all right?" I rounded on her, eyes wild and half shifted. My wolf was close to the surface, threatening to burst free of the man encasing it.

"Gone?" She sensed the threat and backed up several steps. Her fingers clutched the Bone Clan medallion around her neck when the truth of my words hit her. "Why would he do that? We were so close. Everything was prepared."

"I guess close doesn't cut it." I sat on the edge of the bed and pulled a pair of thick wool socks over my scabbed feet. The cuts from the broken glass were all but healed. "Now, are you going to help me get her back or not?"

"I...I can't help you." Her gaze flicked about the room, settling on the destruction in the bathroom.

She must have assumed the damage had been done by Darius because she had a sudden change of heart. I didn't bother to correct her.

"What do you need me to do?" Valerie opened the hope chest at the foot of the bed and rummaged through its contents, tossing a pair of gloves, scarf and knit hat onto the mattress.

"I need you to help me get out of Boot Hill and back to Dead Horse. I'll meet up with my betas, who should be there already, and start looking for her." I stripped one of the pillows of their silk cover and stuffed the extra gloves and scarf inside before pulling the knit hat over my head.

As far as disguises went, it was pitiful, but I made do with what I had and hoped it helped me to blend in.

"Your betas?" Valerie asked with a bewildered look on her face as she rolled the word around in her mouth, seeming to process what I said. "You and Talia took the last trip out of Dead Horse when Lincoln brought you here. The pilots grounded their planes, Bjorn's orders. I don't know where your betas are, but it isn't in Dead Horse."

"Damn it." So much for Plan A. I'd hoped to get back to town, meet up with Markus, Theo and David to regroup and search for Talia.

It looked like I was on my own without a Plan B.

"What are you going to do? You're not one of us, Galen. Your kind aren't built for the cold. Not the way demon wolves are. You won't last five minutes if you shift out there." Valerie mashed her lips into a thin line and rested her hands on her hips. "Don't be rash. You can't save her if you're dead."

"I can't save her if I'm stuck here." I pulled on my coat and zipped it up with more force than necessary.

The irony of a demon wolf clan being better equipped for subzero temperatures and life on a frozen tundra, given the association with their forebears and hotter climates was not lost on me.

Still, she wasn't wrong.

If I survived the daylight hours, when the sun fell and the temperatures dropped even further, I was dead, and Talia was mated to a demon wolf god.

A knock on the door pierced the awkward silence that had fallen between us.

"Valerie?" A muffled male voice came from the other side of the door. "Bjorn is getting impatient. Where's Talia? Open the door."

"It's Vincent. What if he heard us?" Valerie's eyes widened and her brows hit her hairline as she mouthed the words. She shook her head, her braid swishing behind her. "I can't help you. I'm sorry."

She took a deep breath, switched gears from what appeared to be a genuine fear of being caught aiding and abetting the princess' consort in his escape, to panic stricken and rushed for the door.

"Victor, thank the gods you're here." She clutched her brother's arm and dragged him into the room. "She's gone. Talia's gone. What do we do? What are we going to tell Bjorn?"

She played the part well, though the actual events that had unfolded minutes before she arrived helped inspire and really sell her performance.

"What? What do you mean gone?" A cloud of red swallowed the irises of Victor's eyes. His wolf was near the surface and ready to pounce.

"He said someone took her. A servant of our lord and master, another demon wolf named Darius." Valerie extended her well-toned arm and pointed her long, graceful finger at me as if I were the guilty party in Talia's disappearance.

I was innocent of her kidnapping... this time. But that didn't stop the guilt of my failure to protect my mate from making me feel complicit. Fate wielded irony like a club and continued to bash me over the head with it.

"Darius? Wasn't he a member of your pack?" Victor had done his homework on the Long Claws, no doubt scouting us for Bjorn after we returned home from the Alliance summit. "In a high-ranking position among your wolves? Please, don't insult my intelligence. It's a ruse, and a poor one at that."

"Victor, I don't think it is." Valerie shoved her brother into the bathroom, showing him the destruction and the faint trace of the shadow portal Darius conjured stained onto the far wall adjacent to the shower stall. "Look, there. Do you see it? The outline... it's right there."

"We're taking him to Bjorn. Now." Victor rounded on me, narrowing his gaze as if daring me to argue.

I didn't take the bait. At that point, the Alpha was my only way out of the encampment. The longer I was stuck in Boot Hill, the further away I was from finding Talia.

"What are we waiting for?" I grabbed what little spare clothing I had and shoved it in the pillowcase, hitching over my shoulder. "After you."

Victor stormed out the bedroom door with his sister hot on his heels and me bringing up the rear. They ushered me from Talia's room, down a long corridor to the side of the building where the Alpha's living quarters were located.

Victor's fist hovered over the door, poised to knock, but it appeared he needed a moment to compose himself before doing so.

"Pray to the gods he doesn't take his wrath out on us."

The Alpha beckoned us into his rooms before Victor had a chance to announce our presence.

"Where's Talia?" Bjorn scratched his bearded jaw and leaned back in a chair draped with fur pelts, the old wood creaking in protest.

On the surface, he appeared relaxed, calm waters belying the tsunami building in the depths below. I recognized the look in his eyes and the anger simmering within him. Bjorn and I were nothing alike but at that moment with the weight of

Talia's kidnapping bearing down on us, we could have been identical twins.

"She's gone, Alpha." Valerie dropped to her knees and bent at the waist in a deep bow until her forehead pressed against the floor.

"Galen claims a wolf from his pack—"

"Darius." Bjorn leveled Victor with a soul-piercing gaze forcing the wolf to submit and mirror his sister's pose. "A spy in the service of our god."

"You knew he was planning to take her?" My hands curled into fists at my side, the rage roiling inside me threatening to boil over. "And you didn't even try to stop him? What about your ceremonies and all the other sanctimonious bullshit? What the fuck was all that for if you were just going to let Darius drag her away?"

"I knew that a spy had planted himself among your pack and put two and two together when Victor reported back with your roster. If Talia didn't come to us willingly, his job was to... persuade her." Bjorn rested his elbows on his knees and steepled his fingers together. "It seems this other demon wolf, Darius, wanted the glory of bringing our god his bride for himself. Talia's where she belongs. How she got there is of no consequence to me."

"And now that he has her, what do you plan to do with me?" My wolf stalked to the surface, his claws raking my insides as he tried to break free.

But I couldn't afford to lose control.

Every second I spent with Bjorn was time wasted. Time that I needed to save Talia from being forced into matrimony with their demon wolf god.

"I have no further use for you, Galen Long Claw. You served your purpose. You're free to go." Bjorn's mouth curved into a treacherous sneer.

"Alpha?" Victor inched his head up and peered at the leader of his pack in question.

"He won't survive the elements, and the blood of an Alpha outside of a challenge won't be on our hands should the Alliance decide to question us. Release him." Bjorn gave his final word and concluded the conversation with a wave of his hand.

We'd been dismissed.

Victor rose and extended his hand to his sister, helping to her feet. They each took a place at my side and ushered me out of the room.

"You take only what you have on you." Victor stepped out in front and led us down another hallway that led to the airlock door.

"Good luck." Valerie rested her hand on my shoulder before turning me loose. "You'll need it."

Her brother's expression darkened, as if her words were treasonous but otherwise kept his thoughts to himself.

The Deofol Alpha said I was free to go, and I didn't need to be told twice. I bolted out of the door, my head dipped down away from the bitter wind, without as much as a goodbye or good riddance.

No one tried to stop me as I made my way across the encampment.

I moved at a good clip, careful not to build up a sweat and increase my risks of hypothermia, slowing once to eavesdrop on a conversation between two guards about a string of demon attacks from Boot Hill, through Dead Horse, Wiseman and Cold Foot.

Darius' appearance and the demons couldn't have been a coincidence. I picked up my pace and mapped out the site of the attacks in my head. They seemed to be leading back to Anchorage.

I didn't have a plan but I had a destination. However, there was no way I would make it there in time. Not on foot and not in a truck—at least not the whole way.

One step at a time.

Bjorn issued one last order upon my release. No one in Boot Hill was permitted to help me. So, I helped myself instead—to one of their vehicles.

After pulling and twisting a few wires and with the help of a flat head screwdriver from the toolbox on the passenger side floorboard, I got the old F-150 running. The snow chains on the tires made tearing out of Boot Hill and pursuing Darius a hell of a lot easier.

It wasn't difficult to pick up his trail. All I had to do was follow the bodies. Talia had uncovered the reason behind the demon attacks in the lower forty-eight, but I couldn't understand why there were so many casualties between the Deofol pack lands and Anchorage.

But I lost them just outside the city limits.

The body count dropped, and the trail went cold. The temperatures, on the other hand, were up. Which meant my wolf could aid in the search. Without a home base to resupply, clothes and all, after each shift, I needed to be more strategic and that was something neither of us were used to.

I relied on my wolf and the ability to shift whenever I needed or wanted to.

Finding a place to stash the truck and dividing what little supplies I had into a couple of caches in the woods as I searched was my best option. I veered off road where the snowpack was shallow enough to drive in, pulled off in the woods and used downed limbs to camouflage the truck as best I could.

After salvaging everything useful from inside the cab, I split my gear into two caches, stripped down and called my wolf. My shift came on hard and fast. He was as eager to find Talia as I was.

Nose to the ground, we scoured the area for any trace scent of our mate and the traitorous bastard who'd taken her from us. The overpowering smell of sulfur permeated the snow-covered ground, but underneath the rank demon stench was a hint of honeysuckle.

Talia.

The hunt was on. We blocked out everything else and zeroed in on her scent. Darius had at least an hour's head start on me, but I was closing in. And when I found him, he was a dead man. I hoped for his sake his demon wolf god was merciful, because I would not be.

I ran faster, harder than I ever had in my life, pushing my wolf to his limits without the pack to draw power from. But if I wasn't careful, I'd drain myself dry, leaving me in a vulnerable position when I caught up with Darius.

And that was a mistake I couldn't afford to make.

He needed to be taken out of the equation and fast because I had a feeling that when Bjorn found out I'd opted for stealing a truck and going after my mate rather than die on the ice like he'd planned, the Deofol pack would be breathing down my neck.

That is, if the demon horde at Darius' command didn't find me first.

# CHAPTER 2
# TALIA

"Get your filthy hands off me." I clawed, kicked and bit, struggling to break free of Darius' iron grip as he dragged me deeper into the shadows and into the portal he'd conjured to transport us from Boot Hill to... wherever the hell we were.

"We'll stay here for the night." Darius ripped back a veil of shadows and revealed a gaping hole in the hillside. "Get some rest. You'll need it. We leave for my lord's temple at sunrise. This time tomorrow you'll be the new wife of a god."

"He should pay more attention to his old wife." I raised my knee up and reared back, connecting my heel between Darius's legs with a meaty thud.

He grunted and groaned, but his grip never slackened.

"I have killed people for less than that." He grabbed my free hand and chicken-winged it behind my back to match my other arm.

"Go ahead, you worthless piece of scum. Kill me." Antagonizing the demon wolf god's henchman was probably a terrible idea, but I couldn't seem to help myself. "Oh, wait. You can't kill me."

"You're right. I can't." He shoved me forward hard enough to make me stumble forward but jerked me back before I could fall. "But make no mistake, Princess, I can still hurt you."

My shoulder popped out of socket and sent an arc of pain from the joint to the tips of my fingers. I bit down on the inside of my cheek until I tasted blood to keep myself from screaming. I refused to give Darius the satisfaction.

"I don't think your so-called god wants a bruised and beaten bride. Do you?" I choked out, hoping he'd release me before my enhanced ability to heal kicked in and reconstructed the ligaments with my arm twisted at an odd angle only for me to have it dislocated and reset so it could heal properly later.

"You know what they say…Something old, something new. Something borrowed, something *blue*." Darius shoved me again, forcing me down a dark, damp tunnel carved into the hillside that opened up into a large cavern. "There won't be a mark on you when you meet your husband for the first time."

My stomach threatened to turn itself inside out at the thought of my upcoming nuptials. The only vows I'd planned on taking were with Galen. I needed to come up with an escape plan. *Again*.

It felt like I'd been running from something since the day I was born. My mother's past, my father's misdeed, their deaths, the Northwood pack. Hell, even my own blood with its demon wolf lineage traced back to the Bone Clan had me on the run. I was sick and tired of running, but I couldn't stop.

Not yet. Not until I was away from Darius, and back in Galen's arms.

My best chance at escape was when Darius fell asleep. *If* he fell asleep. His ability to pull on the shadows and bend them to his will led me to believe he was more demon than wolf. Or not a wolf at all, but a demon using black magic to disguise himself as a wolf, infiltrate the Long Claw pack and gain Galen's trust.

The latter seemed to be the most likely scenario.

Candles adhered to stalagmites and stalactites with melted wax illuminated the cavern. Two insulated sleeping bags had been rolled out onto the dirt floor, one on either side of a small fire ring in the center of the room. It wasn't hard to guess which sleeping bag was mine.

Because it certainly wasn't the one nearest the tunnel.

The cavern had one point of egress, and Darius made sure to position himself between me and the exit. Which made escaping difficult, but not impossible.

"These are for your ceremony tomorrow." He pulled a gauzy white skirt and matching bustier from inside a leather backpack beside his sleeping bag and threw the outfit at me. "Try it on and see if it fits."

The ankle-length skirt had high slits on both sides that ran to the top of the thigh and the bustier had less fabric than some of my best bras.

"I think he has me confused with another princess. I'm not interested in indulging his galactic science fiction fantasies." I tossed the clothes on the fire, stepping back from the plume of smoke with a satisfied smirk. "I may be a princess, but I'm not that princess."

"You can wear nothing for all I care." Darius's lips curled up in an evil sneer, exposing the tips of his elongated canines. "I'm sure he would prefer you that way."

Regret ate away at my smile as the flames consumed the skimpy wedding clothes he'd provided. Even a scrap of fabric covering my body from the demon wolf god's eyes would have been better than nothing.

"That's what I thought." Darius fished another option from his bag and held it out to me. "Before you get any more bright ideas, you should know after this one, you're out of options."

I stormed over to his side of the earthen chamber and snatched the dress out of his hands. The sheer fabric with plunging neckline and hip high slits left little to the imagination, but it was a far cry better than being forced to marry the demon wolf god in the nude.

"Turn around." I draped the garment over my forearm and crossed my arms over my chest. "I'm not stripping in front of you."

"Don't worry, princess. I have no interest in sampling the goods before my lord has his fill." He raked his gaze over my body, violating me without as much as placing a finger on my body. "There will be plenty of opportunities for that when he grows tired of you."

"You're disgusting." I didn't think it was possible to hate my title any more than I already did, but every time he called me princess, I loathed the word a little bit more.

"Maybe so, but I'm not stupid." Darius mirrored my stance, arms folded over his chest, and barked out a bitter laugh. "If you think I'm going to turn the other way, exposing my back and giving you an opportunity to attack me from behind, you are crazier than I thought."

"That's rich, coming from you." I snap, seething over his implication that of the two of us I'm the crazy one. "You don't see me kidnapping innocent women and throwing them at the mercy of some evil entity."

"You have been chosen as a mate for a god and *you would choose a mere Alpha wolf?* That sounds pretty insane to me." Darius levels me with a glare that would have had me quaking in my boots had I been wearing any. His hands clench at his sides. "My patience is wearing thin, Princess. I have to deliver you to my lord in the morning, but I promise these will be the longest hours of your life if you don't start doing as you're told. Try. On. The. Dress."

Something flashes in his eyes, a look that says he's close to making good on his threats, and while I know he won't kill me, I have no desire to find out how close he's willing to get to that line before crossing it.

I needed to escape. Something I wouldn't be able to do if I pushed him to his breaking point. We were below the arctic circle, but the climate and terrain weren't any more forgiving. My chances of survival in the elements after I made my move were already low. I couldn't let my pride get in my way.

I swallowed past the lump in my throat and pivoted on my left heel, turning my back on Darius, and uncinched the robe's tie around my waist. After stepping into the dress and inching it up over my hips, I shrugged off the robe and slipped my arms through the spaghetti straps, securing them over my shoulders.

"It fits." I knelt down, grabbed the robe, slipped it back on over the dress and cinched the tie around my waist before turning back around.

"At this point, I'll take your word for it." Darius relaxed his fists once I complied with his demands, but his attitude and body language were as rigid as ever. He pointed to the sleeping bag opposite his. "All the comforts of home. Sleep. You'll need your strength tomorrow."

I didn't press him for details on why I'd need my strength. The remainder of the trip, the ceremony? I shuddered. The wedding night? All of the above?

It didn't matter because he was right about needing my strength, but all his reasons as to why would have been wrong.

I needed every ounce of strength and energy I could muster to run.

"Don't worry, Princess." Darius dragged his sleeping bag across the entrance into the tunnel and settled in with his legs outstretched and his back pressed against one wall. "You'll be safe in here with me keeping watch until sunrise. Sweet dreams."

"You have to sleep sometime," I grumbled to myself, opting to sleep on top of the sleeping bag for less noise and a quick getaway.

I laid on my side facing the back wall of the cavern and pretended to drift off, relaxing and slowing the pattern of my breathing to simulate falling asleep. But the only person in danger of succumbing to exhaustion was me.

Darius seemed as alert as ever. His eyes were wide and bright and his breathing steady. Perhaps his demon blood gave him an edge and he didn't need sleep the way we did. Whatever it was, it seemed I would have to wait a long time for an opportunity to escape to present itself.

It was up to me to make one.

I laid there wrapped in the sleeping bag and ran through

ways to distract Darius and make my escape. My options were limited and by limited, I meant nonexistent.

The bond between Galen and me had been blocked for days, but I reached out in the hope that he could hear me. I could feel him through our connection but couldn't hear his thoughts. Still, I tried communicating anyway with the hope that something would get through. I sent a reassuring message that I was unharmed and gave him my best guess as to our location. I felt a vibration in the bond.

Except, it wasn't Galen.

The resonance was different. It felt a little bit like Galen, as if part of him was there. I recognized his spiritual signature, but there was something else. Something more. I focused on the sensation, the pieces moving through our bond that were different from my mate and tried to pinpoint what or who it originated from.

I clamped my hand over my mouth to stifle a gasp. I fought through the initial shock and disbelief, clearing my mind of all that useless noise until all that remained was the source. It was still there. The more I concentrated, the more familiar it became.

Me.

It wasn't two separate energies that I felt, but one. A combination of Galen and me. But that was impossible... or very improbable. *Wasn't it?* The odds of getting pregnant so soon? Our relationship was hardly what the shifter community would consider consummated.

The animalistic nature of our werewolf blood drove our need to mate and procreate, but it never seemed as easy as just claiming a mate for the women in the Northwood pack. There were fewer with each year that passed, which led to other methods of expansion.

There was no denying the combination I felt, a mix of me and Galen. But was it our mating bond taking hold? Would I bear his mark along with the demon wolf god's? Or something more?

I couldn't afford to get my hopes up. Not for a bond, and especially not for a baby. Not when so much was riding on my freedom.

On my future with Galen.

The cost of losing either of those possibilities would have been more than I could bear. So, I did the only thing I could— forget about my happily ever after with Galen and focus all my energy on getting away from Darius and the clutches of his master.

My future with Galen went hand in hand with my freedom. I couldn't have one without the other, but it was clear which came first. I had to keep my head and my priorities straight if I wanted to defeat Darius.

And losing was not an option.

I'd bested more than one Alpha. First in a physical fight against the Northwood Alpha and then a battle of wits against the Alpha of the Deofol pack. Not to mention the priceless information I gained after convincing Valerie that I intended to go along with their plans.

The demon wolf goddess was my golden ticket, the answer to all my problems. I just needed to get to her, to prove to her that I'm not her enemy and wanted nothing to do with her husband.

That conversation wasn't going to happen if I just sat on

my ass and did nothing. I had to try.

I called my wolf, gathered what little added strength I could from my mating bond with Galen and shifted. The borrowed energy provided enough of a boost to reduce the pain and speed up the process of my transformation. Darius never noticed I'd changed.

Until it was too late.

"You think you can take me?" He leapt to his feet, spreading his arms and widening his stance to block the exit.

My lips curled back, exposing two rows of deadly teeth. A growl built in the back of my throat, and I gave myself over to the primal instincts of my wolf.

"Little Princess wants to play?" Darius taunted me, a malevolent sneer darkening his expression. "Come on, Snow White, let's see what you can do. We've got all night."

Bones snapped and cracked out of joint as he succumbed to the change from man to demon wolf. His skin splintered, peeling away to reveal thick obsidian fur coated in an oily sheen. Dingy, yellow claws scraped away the last remnants of the person who'd stood before me moments before.

This version of Darius's wolf was different from the one I saw when he pretended to be a lone wolf and infiltrated the Long Claw pack. He showed his true nature, proving that he was more demon than wolf.

Darius didn't drop on all four and move like a wolf. He stood erect, on hind legs like a man. Saliva dripped from his lower jaw. When he tipped his head back and howled, I knew I'd underestimated my opponent.

I'd made a mistake, but it was too late to change course.

The look in Darius' eyes confirmed it. I'd pushed him too

far. Even if I'd submitted and shifted back to my human form, the demon that rode him would not accept surrender. It wanted blood, and my ability to heal assured that he could have it.

He stalked forward, claws scratching and chipping away at the dirt floor with each step. He lashed out, swiping with his left hand. I dodged right, narrowly avoiding what would have been a bone cracking blow to my ribs. Deadly nails grazed my coat and my white fur fell to the ground like a dusting of fresh snow.

Darius howled again and feigned a hit from his right. I took the bait, dodged left and moved into the path of a solid left-handed blow to my side. I yelped and slid across the cavern. My nails raked the floor as I tried to regain purchase and avoid smashing into the rock wall.

I bit back a yowl, refusing to give him the satisfaction of knowing he'd hurt me and pushed myself to my feet. My side felt like it was on fire and every breath I drew caused an arc of searing pain across my abdomen. I tried to take stock of my injuries, but there wasn't enough time for triage or treatment in the midst of a fight.

Especially against a demon wolf hybrid as strong as Darius.

Despite my efforts to hide the pain, it was obvious I was injured. He sensed my weakness and moved in for a series of knock-out, fight ending blows. The first connected with the side of my jaw and cracked my canine tooth. I collapsed, trapped between Darius and the back wall of the cavern.

He curled his fingers, extended the razor-sharp claws at the end of his fingers and coiled his arm back. I wasn't sure if he planned to stab or slice, but either would have left me bloodied and with muscle damage.

He'd warned me not to test him, that just because he couldn't kill me didn't mean he couldn't cause me a great deal of pain.

I thought about the sensation I'd felt through the mating bond with Galen, that odd combination of both our energies. What if I really was pregnant? If Darius gutted me, I might not die, but I'd lose my baby.

Galen's baby.

That was all the motivation I needed to push myself back to my feet. *Keep fighting, Talia. Stay alive. Break free.* I repeated it over and over, until I was up on all fours. I used the only advantage I had over a demon wolf hybrid. My size.

I darted between his legs and clawed his Achilles tendon. Darius staggered forward but the slash to the back of his ankles wasn't enough to take him down. He pivoted, reached back, and grabbed the tip of my tail.

"Bitch," he growled, dangling me upside down in front of him.

Snarling and growling, I curled up and bit down on his wrist. Thick, acrid blood filled my mouth, but I held on and forced my jaws together. He howled in pain. A chunk of flesh was torn from his arm as he shook me off.

I spat the blood, skin and muscle at his feet and bolted for the tunnel that led out to the Alaskan wilderness and my freedom.

Darius recovered and pounded down the narrow passageway, gaining ground with each step he took. I pushed myself harder and ran faster than I ever had toward the flicker of moonlight at the end of the tunnel.

Something moved in the distance, snuffing out the light and submerging us in darkness. Darius's distorted laughter sent a chill down my spine and raised the hackles on the back of my neck. I felt the thunder of his steps vibrate beneath my feet, the heat of his breath on my hide, but I never looked back.

I kept running, charging toward whatever blocked my path to freedom.

# CHAPTER 3

# GALEN

Talia was close. I'd picked up her scent. It was faint, and tainted by Darius's rank odor, but I managed to track them through the woods to the entrance of a den carved out in the hillside. The closer I came, the stronger the connection was through our bond. I felt her for the first time since Bjorn held us hostage and tampered with it, cutting off our communication.

Something I hadn't even known was possible.

Perhaps their demon wolf god taught them things wolves in the lower forty-eight had long since forgotten in exchange for their worship and obedience. Or it could have been black magic, a spell they'd purchased from a dark witch as part of their plan to capture Talia.

Back in the Deofol encampment, I'd spent the hours trapped in my cage trying to work out how Bjorn broke the connection. I was terrified the damage to the bond had been permanent, but I didn't care how he did it, not anymore. Our connection had been restored and the ache, that void left behind when the mating bond with Talia had been severed, was gone. Talia was back.

And she was in trouble.

I felt the beat of her racing heart, the searing pain that arced through her body, the burn in her lungs with each panting breath she took. She was injured, on the run and headed straight for me.

"Talia!" I called her name and reached through the bond, letting her know I was there and that everything was going to be okay now that we were together again.

"Galen, run!"

Talia and I were on a collision course as she barreled toward me, breaking right at the last second as she exited the mouth of the cave to avoid ramming into me. "It's Darius. He's—"

Her fear came through the bond and hit me like a hurricane a second before the monstrosity that was Darius's wolf burst out of the entrance of the den behind her. He exploded out of the hillside in a hail of dirt and rock, looking unlike any wolf I'd seen, natural or supernatural. He'd shifted into a creature straight out of a Hollywood horror film.

"Get behind me." I pulled on the pack bonds, borrowing as much energy as I could siphon over the vast distance that separated me from the Long Claw wolves.

Talia was never one to take orders.

She was a worthy mate, a true match for the Alpha I hoped to be. She refused to stand at my back and joined me at my side to face our enemy.

"He won't stop, Galen. I thought I could take him, but he's

stronger than I realized." She clawed the snow-covered earth and hunched down, ready to lunge at Darius. "I think his half demon nature gives him an edge."

"Don't worry. He's not walking out of here." I mirrored her stance and prepared to attack. "Wait for the dust to settle. We need to see him. On my count. One...two..."

The Deofol pack and their demon wolf god were wrong about my mate. Talia wasn't meant to be crowned with a tiara and locked away in a tower. She was a warrior. A shieldmaiden, destined for the battlefield.

But instead of a sword or spear, she was armed with teeth and claws.

"Three." I gave the signal, coordinating our plan of attack through the bond.

I went right and Talia went left, flanking him from both sides. Darius' eyes widened. It seemed he'd been so focused on Talia that he hadn't realized I was there until it was too late. With his attention divided, we were able to amplify the damage we inflicted.

Darius shook Talia off, and I went to work, latching onto his arm, gnawing at muscle and sinew. He grabbed the scruff of my neck and ripped me off his forearm like a bandage, but Talia was back, her teeth sinking to the gums into his calf. He kicked her off with his free leg, and I jumped back into the fray.

We tag-teamed the attack, taking turns landing hits and taking blows, until we wore him down. Darius collapsed in a pool of his own blood. The drops, splatters and splotches, mimicked a Pollock painting, destroying the pristine beauty of untouched snow.

I limped over to the traitor's side, pressed my muzzle

against his neck and checked for a pulse. Nothing. I waited, watching his chest for any sign of breathing, and checked again. Still nothing.

The demon wolf god was down one disciple. Darius was dead.

"Do you think he can come back?" Talia asked through the bond and nuzzled her nose into my fur.

"I have no idea, but we probably shouldn't hang around to find out. Especially since Bjorn and the rest of the Deofol pack are probably hot on my trail." I gave her a brief rundown of how I'd been released, and the demon wolf pack's Alpha's assumptions that I'd die from exposure, tying off any loose ends without getting his hands bloodied. "The truck I borrowed isn't far from here."

"We need to shift to heal first. Probably more than once. We can't afford to run into Bjorn or another demon-wolf hybrid while we're healing wounds from our fight with the last one." She turned and headed back toward the cave. "There's a fire, and I've got a change of clothes inside the cavern. Come on."

I followed her into the mouth of the cave and down the dark passageway to a large cavern. It was taller and wider on the inside than I'd expected. The fire clung to life, smoldering wood and coals that were left in the rock circle.

"Looks like there are a few supplies here we can use." I'd completed my first shift and rooted through the items Darius left behind.

Talia did the same, shifting out of her wolf form and into the beautiful woman who'd taken my breath away and claimed my heart the first time I laid eyes on her.

"We don't have time for that." A blush warmed Talia's

cheeks when she caught me staring at her naked form. Her gaze drifted down my body, admiring the physical evidence of how attracted I was to her. There was a promise of things to come in her smile. "We don't have time...right now."

I pulled her into my arms, pressed my lips to hers and claimed her mouth. She deepened the kiss, her tongue slipping past my lips, exploring my mouth. Her passion set my soul on fire. My fingers trailed up her back, skimming her bare skin, before I buried them in the silky, golden tresses at the base of her neck.

Fuck, I wanted her. Needed her. But she was right. We didn't have time.

"But when we do..." I made promises of my own, to worship every inch of her body and ravish her properly at the first opportunity.

We shifted once more and warmed our fur by the fire while the transformation process healed any injuries that remained. Talia changed one last time and dressed for the walk back to the truck, layering as many clothes as she could find. She packed the rest of the supplies into one of the sleeping bags and hitched it over her shoulder.

Without my clothes I was forced to make the trek back to the truck as a wolf. Even if I had my clothes, I'd have chosen to stay in my wolf form. After all, there were other wolves out there looking for Talia.

We managed to avoid crossing paths with anyone from the Deofol pack and reached the truck, which remained camouflaged under the pile of downed branches. I shifted, got dressed and cleared away the limbs piled over the vehicle.

"Where to?" I opened the passenger door for Talia and helped her climb inside the lifted truck.

"Valerie mentioned the Brooks Range. There's no way to know for sure if she was telling the truth about where the demon wolf goddess lived, but it's the best we've got to go on." Talia adjusted the vents and cranked the heat.

"It's the only thing we've got to go on. Brooks Range it is." I dropped the truck into four-low, eased on the gas and let it crawl out of the snowbank.

We hit the Dalton highway and reached Coldfoot without any sign of the Deofol pack or the demon wolf god's minions. The town was home to less than twenty people and had been razed to the ground. Darius and his demon cohorts left no survivors or any of the service buildings standing.

"They leveled the gas station." I glanced at the fuel gauge on the truck and did some quick math on the miles left on the tank.

It wasn't enough.

"We'll have to hike most of the way, but I don't think we've got enough gas to get to the base of the mountains. We're running on fumes."

Darius hadn't been on a senseless rampage. He'd taken out strategic locations to ensure Talia wouldn't be able to hitch a ride or hop on a plane.

Little did he know we weren't looking for a way out of Alaska. Still, no gas stations proved to be a problem, even for the short distance we needed to travel.

"There's a car over there." Talia pointed to a rusted out Geo Tracker that looked like it hadn't run since the day it rolled off the assembly line thirty-some years ago. "Maybe we could siphon some gas out of the tank."

"If there's gas in it, it's probably no good. But I guess it's worth a shot." I climbed into the back of the truck's cab and rummaged through the toolboxes for anything that I could use to drain the gas out of the old SUV. "There's some hose line in here, I think it's for brake fluid, but it might do the trick."

There was just enough hose to create the vacuum and empty the contents of the Tracker's tank into an old metal gas can I found in the bed of the truck. It was a little thick and smelled off, but bad gas was better than no gas. We didn't have far to go to reach the Gates of the Arctic National Park and our entry point into the Brooks Range. From there we'd hike in and begin our search for the demon wolf goddess.

I hoped she was more reasonable than her husband. Though, based on what we'd seen and heard so far, it seemed highly unlikely.

The engine died a slow and painful death over the last mile of the ride. It took its last gasp and sputtered out a couple hundred feet from the entrance to the gates.

"I almost feel bad for trashing the engine with that gas." I shifted into park and turned the key out of habit. "Almost."

"Well, at least we can see the entrance to the trail from here." Talia reached over the back of her seat and grabbed our coats and gloves. "We better get suited up and start hiking. The sun will be going down before we know it."

We layered up, grabbed the sleeping bag and the rest of our gear and headed out. The surface of the snowpack had crusted over with a thin sheet of ice, making it easier for us to hike across the plains into the foothills and eventually the mountains.

Though I hoped we'd find the goddess before we had to make our ascent. The Brooks Range was unforgiving to the most experienced climbers, and Talia and I did not fall into that category.

"We've got a lot of ground to cover, and need to conserve energy, but I don't like you being out in the open like this." I was one step behind Talia and a half step to her left to keep an eye out in case we were attacked.

I wouldn't put it past Bjorn, the demon wolf god, or his wife, to try to cut us off at the pass.

We double timed it across the flatland, careful not to break into a sweat and risk hypothermia later and made it to foothills and the cover of the tree line.

"The sun's already going down. We better find some shelter or make some." Talia had been keeping track of our time and distance to ensure we could cover ground and still have enough daylight left to set up camp for the night.

"I doubt we'll find anything, so we'll make use of what we've got." I snapped branches off the pine trees, stripping the smaller limbs, and made a lean-to.

The greens and twigs were used for bedding and kindling. I was fortunate enough to find a piece of fatwood saturated in sap and perfect for starting a fire.

Not that we had anything to cook over it.

There wasn't much in the way of food in the truck or in the forest. The animals were all bedded down for the night, which would have made hunting a waste of time and energy.

I used an old soup can I found in the bed of the truck, boiled snow to clean it as best I could and set about making pine needle tea. It was neither nutritious nor delicious, but it was hot, and enough to curb our appetite for the night.

At least we were warm—and together.

The panic and fear of losing Talia were gone. So was the adrenaline rush. Every bone and muscle in my body ached. I was exhausted after searching for Talia and fighting alongside her to take down Darius, I was mentally and physically exhausted.

But all of that paled when compared to the reality of just how close I'd come to losing her.

My eyes burned and my throat clenched as I choked back emotions that threatened to swallow me whole while watching her warm herself by the fire. Talia had become my whole world. She was more than just Long Claw pack. She was *my* pack. My mate. My home. I would do anything to keep her safe.

And that included facing down a demon wolf god.

"I was so scared we wouldn't find each other again." Talia's eyes glistened with unshed tears. A few threatened to spill over, clinging to her lashes, but she swiped them away with her gloved hand before they fell. "I couldn't hear or feel you through our bond for so long, I thought it was broken."

Talia mirrored my thoughts and as much as I hated to see her so upset, my heart swelled with the affirmation that she felt the same for me as I did for her. She loved me and made me want to be a better man. A better wolf.

"Me too, but I would have never stopped looking for you. Ever." I tossed the pine branches in my hand on the fire and went to her, pulling her in my arms. "You are my mate, Talia. I don't need a mark or ceremony to prove it. You are the air that I breathe, the water I drink, the food I eat. You nourish my soul, and I cannot imagine a life without you in it. I will never give up on you or our life together."

"I love you too." Her tears spilled over her long, lush lashes, crystalizing as they streamed down her cheeks. She wrapped her arms around my waist and nuzzled her face against my neck as she tightened her hold. "I just want this to be over."

"I know, baby. Me, too. And it will be." I pressed a kiss against the top of her head and breathed in her scent.

Our bond reopened, emotions and thoughts flowing both ways for the first time in days. I exhaled the tension coiled inside me when Talia's energy rushed through the connection between us.

"It's back." She sighed and clutched me tighter.

"You know, this whole time I thought it was something Bjorn did. But maybe it was Darius." I eased back out of our embrace enough to look at her.

"And now that he's dead, whatever curse he used to block the bond is lifted?" Talia gnawed at her bottom lip as she tried to puzzle it out. "It's possible. I mean, it makes more sense than Bjorn having a way to do it since Darius had been serving the demon wolf god the whole time."

We'd laid so much of the blame at the feet of the Deofol pack, but it was clear the demon wolf god had more help than we realized.

Some of which was headed straight for us.

"Do you hear that?" I asked, despite knowing that she could. Not just through our bond, but her body language.

"What is it?" Her body tensed and went rigid in my arms.

"I think it's safe to say whatever it is, it's not of the natural world." I let her go, and unzipped my coat, preparing to strip down before I shifted.

Talia did the same, preparing herself for the fight we both sensed was coming.

"They'll try to separate us, to take me out and take you away. No matter what happens, we stay together." I would not lose her again.

We shifted, transforming into our wolves moments before the first demon reached our camp. His friends weren't far behind. Close to a dozen demons descended on our campsite and as predicted, tried to divide and conquer. More than half of them came after me and the rest went after Talia.

But they weren't prepared for her wolf.

They seemed confused to find an animal where a woman should have been standing. They must have assumed we wouldn't risk the elements, opting for more layers of protective clothing to stay warm and prevent frostbite.

That was their first mistake.

The second was to assume that Talia would be easy prey. They tried to close in and circle around her, but she refused to be trapped and lunged at one of the demons on her left.

I had my hands full with seven or eight demons and lost sight of her after that but tracked her movements through our bond. She held her own, taking down two demons while I battled with several more.

It was a melee of teeth and claws. The demons were armed with similar weapons as werewolves, which made the tactics used to fight them in close combat similar to fighting in a challenge or an attack from another pack. We'd had plenty of experience with the latter, thanks to the Northwoods, and put that knowledge to good use.

As much as I hated that Talia's life with me had been one battle after another, I was grateful she'd learned to hold her own and confidence in her ability to fight and defend herself.

One by one, we whittled down the demons, working our way through the horde until we were fighting side by side again and only three remained. The bodies piled up and black, viscous blood stained the white crystalline snow.

"They should have brought more of their friends with them." Talia's thoughts slid through the bond. Her presence in my mind was like bare skin being caressed with lush velvet.

I'd missed the feeling of that connection with her more than I would have thought possible just weeks before.

"They should have," I replied, pawing at the traces of demon blood on my muzzle. "But I'm glad they didn't."

The demon wolf god had underestimated us. A mistake I doubted he would make again. The next time his minions caught up with us, there was certain to be more of them.

But Talia and I had been outnumbered before.

The demon wolf god or his wife could send as many demons after us as they wanted. We'd never stop fighting.

Talia was mine. Nothing or no one would change that.

# CHAPTER 4

# TALIA

We broke camp, doused the fire with snow and grabbed the few items we had to our names. Galen and I agreed that the campsite wasn't safe anymore, and it was time to move on. Traveling in the frigid temperatures over unknown territory in the dark was dangerous, but so was staying in the same spot where we'd been attacked.

"I think I see a spot over there." Galen pointed to a section of the mountain where the rock face jutted out and created an alcove underneath. "We should be safe here for the night."

It wasn't a straight line hike up the side of the mountain to the flat spot beneath the overhang. We climbed a zigzag pattern through trees and rocks protruding through the snow-covered ground. Aches and pains spread through my arms and legs during the hour-long trek. By the time we stopped, the natural stone slab felt more like a memory foam mattress than a rocky bed.

"What about a fire?" I scanned the ground for leaves or limbs, but there wasn't anything in the way of kindling around the alcove.

"We'll have to make do without one. It's probably for the best anyway. A fire will just be a beacon for our location for any demons searching the mountains for you." Galen dropped the sleeping bags with our gear against the side of the rock wall and set up camp. "I've heard if you can't make a fire that body heat is the next best thing."

"The next best thing, huh?" I unrolled one of the sleeping bags, grabbed the other and stuffed it inside, doubling the layers between us and the freezing arctic night air.

"Hey, I'm just repeating what all the survival experts say," Galen teased as he balled up the nylon sacks that previously housed the sleeping bags to use as makeshift pillows. "We should definitely try it. I mean, better safe than sorry, right?"

"Well. If it's a matter of life and death." I dared the frigid temperatures, stripped out of my clothes and slid inside the sleeping bag. "I'm willing to do whatever it takes to ensure our survival."

And in that moment, making love to Galen felt as if it was imperative to my survival.

After everything we'd been through, I needed to be with him in every way possible for a woman and wolf to physically and emotionally bond with her mate. I wanted to feel his body pressed against mine, his skin against my skin. I wanted him inside me, filling me up until the pleasure was too much and every nerve ending in my body exploded in ecstasy.

Galen's clothes hit the ground a second after mine. He slipped into the sleeping bag beside me and zipped it closed.

The warmth of his body enveloped me as he slid his arms around me and pressed our bodies together. We stayed that way for several moments, relishing the heat building between us, the blistering feel of skin on skin.

Desire pooled inside me, building to a fever pitch with the slightest caress of his fingers against the small of my back. It wasn't a night for foreplay. It was a night for claiming, for taking what was mine.

And I would have him. All of him.

I slid my hand between us, over his defined pectorals and chiseled abs, moving lower, searching, seeking the hardened length of silky, smooth skin and muscle throbbing between us. I rubbed my thumb over the tip, slick with precum, and slid down to the sensitive spot along the back stretched tight from his erection. I felt the rock-hard muscle spasm in my hand and I tightened my grip, rubbing hard and eliciting a gasp of pleasure from Galen. His reaction to my touch and the control I had over him turned me on. I wanted more, needed more, to take him in my mouth and taste the very essence of his masculinity, but there wasn't enough space in the sleeping bag.

I let out a frustrated growl, pressed my free hand against his shoulder and ordered him to roll onto his back. The sleeping bag was tight, forcing me to slide over him. My nipples hardened as my breasts rubbed against his chest. Every cell in my body was on fire, my skin hypersensitive. The slightest brush against him felt like a new, erotic adventure. I hooked my leg over his hip and straddled him, rubbing my slick, wet core along the length of his erection.

"Talia." He sucked in a breath between clenched teeth and gripped my hips. His fingers dug into my skin, the pain mixing with pleasure coaxing a moan from deep in my throat. "You're so fucking beautiful."

Galen arched up and laved my breast, grazing his teeth over my taut nipple. He moved to my other breast, licking and sucking as he angled my hips forward and plunged himself inside. He eased out, slowly, ever so slowly, letting me feel every inch of him until just the head of his cock remained before thrusting the full length of himself inside me again.

"Oh, God, yes." I was so close, on the verge of climax, and rolled my hips, grinding against him with enough pressure to take me over the edge of an orgasm. "Oh god. Yes, yes. More."

He reduced me to the most basic words, unable to master anything but the simplest commands to induce pleasure.

But Galen stopped me, his hands still clamped around my hips, fingers curled around and pressed against my ass.

"Not Him." He pulled my breast into his mouth again, rolling my nipple between his teeth and biting just hard enough to heighten that heady mix of pleasure and pain. "You say my name when I'm fucking you."

He drove me down, burying himself inside me again.

"Say my name." He lifted me up, sliding me along the length of his cock. "Say it. I want to hear you say my name when I make you come."

My cries of pleasure had been just that, nothing more or less, but saying the word God must have been enough to conjure an image in his mind of me fulfilling the role of the demon wolf god's wife. It unleashed something in him, something possessive and primal. Something Alpha.

It called to me, woke something animalistic deep inside of me and I wanted more. More of him, more of everything. I couldn't get enough of him, his hands on my skin, the feel of him buried inside me.

"Galen." I fought his hold and thrust back down, grinding against him when he growled with pleasure.

"Again." He tightened his grip, lifted me up and rolled his hips forward when he drove me back down. The pace was fevered, harder, faster than before. "Say it again."

"Galen." My voice was husky and breathing ragged. I was so close. So close, repeating his name, over and over with each thrust. "Galen. Please. Galen."

"That's it. I fucking love the way it sounds when you say my name." He slid his thumb between us, rubbing his thumb against my clit and ripped the orgasm from my body.

I cried out, the ecstasy almost too much to bear, a heady mix of pleasure and pain as he rolled his thumb over sensitive flesh and said his name again. My muscles clenched around him, pulsing and throbbing as the orgasm wound down, only to build into a second wave when Galen bit down on my shoulder and came inside me.

"My mark." His fingers trailed the indentations from his teeth bruised into my skin. "I like the way it looks on you."

"So do I." My limbs turned to jelly, unable to support my weight and I collapsed against him.

I was exhausted but far from satiated. I wasn't sure that I ever would be. My body and soul would never get enough of him.

"It will fade when you shift." Galen combed his fingers through my hair, working the tangled knots at the ends. "I want it to last, to have a mating mark permanently etched on your skin. The way it's supposed to be."

"Then you'll just have to mark me again when it heals." I pressed my lips to his throat, trailing kisses along his neck. "And again, and again and again."

"It looks like it's already starting to heal." He was ready to stake another claim on my body, his erection returning, hardening beneath me. "I'll have to fix that."

He rolled me over onto my back, wedging his way between my thighs and eased the full length of himself inside me.

"Galen," I whispered his name and tipped my head back, exposing the line of my neck and the sensitive skin in a show of vulnerability and trust.

"Mine," he growled, running his tongue along my throat before sinking his teeth in my shoulder again.

We spent the night in the sleeping bag, but there wasn't enough actual sleeping involved for the day ahead. Still, I had no regrets about the way we'd passed the twilight hours. Sleep deprivation was a small price to pay for the hours of pleasure I'd experienced with Galen.

But making love to him wasn't the only thing that kept me awake.

I dozed off in Galen's arms not long after he did, lulled into a light sleep by the rise and fall of his chest and rhythm of his breathing only to be awoken by a series of weird dreams. Each time I closed my eyes and drifted off, the visions returned.

"Morning." He brushed a kiss against my temple and reached for our clothes, dragging them closer before crawling out of the sleeping bag. "You didn't sleep at all?"

"A little." I fisted my hand over my mouth and stifled a yawn.

"But not enough." Galen zipped up his coat and tugged his

knit hat over his head. "I'm going to climb down a little way and see what I can rustle up for breakfast and a fire."

"I'll come with you. Let me get dressed." I pulled the clothes inside the sleeping bag, shivering when the cold fabric brushed against my skin.

"It's okay, stay here and rest. I won't be gone long." He knelt down and pressed a kiss to the top of my head. "I promise."

I wasn't thrilled with the idea of separating. Under normal circumstances, I wouldn't have thought twice about being left alone, but things had been far from normal for Galen and me. We had demons on our tail, and they were closing in.

Still, we'd run out of what little food we scrounged out of the stolen pickup truck and needed to eat. A fire wouldn't hurt either. We were probably hundreds of miles from the nearest coffee shop, but a cup of steaming hot water would go a long way in taking out the chill that settled into my bones once Galen got out of the sleeping bag and took his body heat with him.

"Hurry back." I turned my head, angling for a kiss, and all but sighed when he pressed his lips to mine.

I put on my clothes like it was an Olympic event and I was trying to beat the world record. The cold air stung my exposed skin, and I hurried to cover as much of it up as possible. My fingers bordered on numb by the time I zipped up my coat and slipped on my gloves.

I was done with winter. And the cold. And snow.

When we found the demon wolf goddess and put a stop to her legion and her husband Galen and I were going on a vacation. Somewhere warm, preferably near the equator with an ocean view and drinks with chunks of pineapple stabbed with those little umbrellas.

I wanted to feel the sun on my skin, sand between my toes, and smell the salt in the air on a warm ocean breeze.

Galen kept his promise and returned a short while later with enough kindling and branches for a small fire and a couple grouse.

"They taste like chicken. Or, at least, that's what I've heard. I haven't eaten one myself." Galen shrugged and plucked the feathers from the small birds, preparing to skewer them over the fire while I loosely packed snow in the old soup can for boiled water.

We hunted. It was part of our nature as werewolves, but with so many of us in close proximity, Galen and I were raised in packs that caught and released their prey to preserve local wildlife populations, but in the mountains, we hunted for food.

I picked at the flame broiled wild poultry and tried to recall the details from my dreams. Unable to shake the feeling that they held a deeper meaning, I concentrated on the images conjured by my subconscious.

"What's wrong? Apart from the obvious, I mean. You've hardly touched your food." Galen took notice of my distraction and unfinished meal. "You need to eat, Talia. We haven't taken in nearly enough calories."

"Especially after all the calories we burned last night." I flashed him a heated smile, the warmth spreading over my face —and places lower on my body—as thoughts of our intense lovemaking replaced those of my dreams.

"All the more reason to finish your breakfast." His wink and mischievous smile rekindled my desire, increasing my appetite for things other than cooked grouse, but he was quick to douse the flames that flickered inside me. "Nope. Not until you eat your breakfast and tell me what *else* is on your mind."

"I don't know. It's probably nothing." I pulled a hunk of breast meat from the bone and took a bite, finishing my thought around a mouthful of food. "I had these weird dreams last night and I can't help but think they mean something. It's crazy, right? I'm overthinking it. Or *maybe I'm crazy.*"

"You're not crazy. You knew there was more to the demon mark just like you knew there was more behind the red eyes of your wolf. I think you need to trust your intuition more." Galen sat down, legs crisscrossed beside me and rested his hand on my thigh with a comforting and supportive touch. "Tell me about your dreams."

"I saw her—the demon wolf goddess. She's angry. Furious might be a better word actually, and she's definitely not my biggest fan." I picked off another piece of meat, and forced myself to take a bite, choking down the food before I revealed the worst of my dreams. "She wants to stop her husband from marrying me and she's happy to kill me in order to achieve her objective."

"You saw all of that in your dreams?" Galen's eyes widened, not in disbelief but in fear.

I could tell by the worry lines around his eyes and deepening creases in his brow.

"I told you." I sighed, and rested my head in my hands, covering my face to hide my embarrassment. "It sounds even crazier now that I've said it out loud."

"Talia." Galen tugged at my hands, moving them from my face and tipping my chin until I met his gaze. "It doesn't sound crazy. But it does sound like we need to rethink our plan. If she's even half as dangerous as you say, we can't just go marching in, demanding her help."

"I don't know about your plan, but mine involved a lot of begging," I joked, adding a meager laugh that didn't quite reach the levity I'd been aiming for.

"Maybe groveling? On your hands and knees" He leaned in and rested his forehead against mine. "That might work. Or we could put our heads together and figure something out."

"The only thing I have to convince her to help us is the truth. I don't want to have anything to do with the demon wolf god. I have a life of my own and a mate. There isn't a single part of my future that involves her husband." I closed the small distance between us and claimed his mouth with a kiss.

"Well, you certainly have me convinced." Galen brushed his nose against mine before pulling away to get up and douse the dwindling fire with handfuls of snow. "Now, all we have to do is find her."

He watched the plume of smoke drift away from the alcove, over the treetops below and into the cloudy horizon, as if it would somehow mark a trail from our campsite to the demon wolf goddess' home.

"I think I already know where she is." My attempt at a smile felt more like a grimace. "At least in my dream, I did."

"You saw where she lives? That's more than we had to go on a few hours ago." Galen rounded on me, clasping his hands and rubbing them together.

He seemed eager if not excited by my announcement. I wished I felt the same way. Apprehension set in like a stone in my stomach.

"Yeah, but why would she do that? Why lead me to her instead of leading her demons to me?" I raised my hands in frustration and let them drop back down into my lap. "It doesn't make sense, unless—"

"Unless she's creating the opportunity she needs." Galen softened the blow, and refrained from saying what I already knew.

The goddess wanted me to go to her. She must have grown tired of the cat and mouse game and wanted to put an end to her problem—namely me—once and for all.

"And you still want to go through with this?" Galen knelt down, wrapped his arms around me and clutched me to his chest. "We got away from Bjorn and the Deofol pack, we eliminated Darius. You don't have to do this. We can run. We'll disappear, drop off the grid and go somewhere they can't find us."

"You're a born Alpha, Galen. You've never run from a challenge in your life, and you're not turning your back on the Long Claw pack or your responsibilities to them. Not because of me. I won't let you." I fought back the sobs brought on by refusing his offer that threatened to break free. "Running sounds like a good idea now, and you'll do it because you're my mate, but over time you'll grow to resent me. Look at the mess I've dragged you into. The price of loving me is too high."

"I'll pay it. I'd pay any ransom, no matter how much, if it meant I still had a future with you." He leaned back, cupped my face in his hands and wiped away my tears with a brush of his thumb. "I am proud to be the Alpha of the Long Claw pack, but if I had to choose, I'd choose you. Every time, I'd choose you, Talia."

"But what if the price is more than the possibility of a future? What if all of this, escaping the demon wolf clan, defying their god and asking a murderous goddess for help… what if the cost of all of that is you? Us?" I clenched my trembling hands together and wrung them in my lap.

"It won't." Galen's tone brooked no argument, but that didn't stop me from raising one.

"You don't know that. There's no guarantee—"

"Fate didn't bring us together only to tear us apart now." Galen separated my hands, placed them flat on my lap and traced a semi-circle on the ring finger of my left hand with his fingertip. "You're my mate, which is a lifetime commitment, and I intend to spend a lifetime with you."

"Okay," was all I managed to say.

There was no changing his mind. No turning back. We were going to face the demon wolf goddess together, and she was going to help us.

Whether she liked it or not.

# CHAPTER 5

# GALEN

Talia had visions. She called them dreams, but we'd both spent enough time around witches in the weeks prior to know the difference. Were they a byproduct of her demon marks and a deepening connection to the demon wolf god who'd wanted to claim her, a latent skill she'd inherited from a mother she never knew made active by the stress we were under, or was the demon wolf goddess somehow invading Talia's mind?

I wasn't a betting man, but if I had to wager, my money was on the latter.

The demon wolf goddess was screwing with us, baiting us into a trap and we had no choice but to walk right into it. Talia felt certain the goddess wanted to kill her and based on what we'd learned, I was inclined to believe her.

Hell hath no fury like a woman scorned. The demon wolf goddess had certainly been scorned, and she'd chosen to unleash her fury on Talia rather than the one who betrayed her. I suppose we made for an easier target than her husband.

The goddess had revealed her location to Talia. Truth be told, I wasn't sure we would have found her in the wilds of Alaska on our own. The backcountry was vast and unforgiving, with plenty of places for the demon wolf goddess to hide her lair.

"Ready?" Talia started packing, stuffing most of our gear into the sleeping bag's carrying case and sliding the plastic lock down the drawstring.

I wanted to ask if *she was* ready, but I already knew the answer.

"To climb down from the relative safety of our camp and face down a powerful and pissed off goddess?" I paused for a little comedic effect and gave her a wink. "Absolutely. I'm just waiting on you."

"Then make yourself useful and help me pack up. The sooner we're done, the sooner we're on the road." She was calm and confident for someone who could lose her life before lunch.

I wish I felt the same.

My insides were twisted up in knots, and I was terrified of losing her. If things went wrong, the demon wolf goddess would capture or kill her. Still, if we did nothing, I'd lose her anyway, to the demon wolf god instead. It felt like a lose-lose scenario.

And it was still our best bet.

We worked our way down the mountain and picked up the trail, well-worn and visible even with the layers of snowfall. The hike out was difficult. We took our time, trudging through snow that was calf deep in some spots. After all, why rush and risk injury when we were already on our way to our potential demise?

The irony was not lost on me.

"Galen?" Talia stopped walking and sniffed the air, picking up a scent.

"I smell them." It was impossible not to. The demons reeked of sulfur and brimstone. "They've been tracking us for the last mile and a half."

They'd stayed down wind of us, but every once in a while the breeze shifted and carried a whiff of their foul odor.

"Can we outrun them? Maybe if we got off the trail, we could lose them in the forest." Talia scanned the woods, searching for an alternate path.

"In these conditions? We'll lose time we don't have by veering off course." I dropped the makeshift pack with our gear and peeled off my clothes one layer at a time. "We'll have to take them out here."

Talia followed my lead, removing her clothes in preparation for the shift, and called on the magic inherent in all shifters. Her wolf's white fur blended into our surroundings. The pristine snow was the perfect camouflage. If not for her red eyes, she would have all but disappeared.

Something we could use to our advantage.

"Use that snow drift over there by that stand of pine trees for cover. When the demons get here, flank them from the right." I waited a breath for her to respond before calling my wolf and giving myself over to the shift.

The transformation came slower and with more pain than

it should have, but I was running on empty. I'd tapped myself out more than once healing injuries sustained at the hands of the Deofol pack, and each time my energy refilled, the well was lower than before.

I'd been away from my pack for too long and there were too many miles between us to borrow the resources I needed through my connection with them. It was an experience I needed to become accustomed to. If things went south, forcing Talia and me to go on the run, I would be forced to abdicate my position as Alpha and lose that ability altogether.

For Talia, I would give that up and more.

I watched her dash for the pines and vanish into the snow. Her wolf was in its natural element. On the outside, Talia was a winter wolf. She was made for the ice and snow, but on the inside, she was all Long Claw.

And she was made for me.

The demons came. There were only four by my count. I'd expected more. Talia and I had faced greater numbers and odds back home. They used their massive size and weight to their advantage, plowing through the snow with ease, and kicked up sprays of the dry, powdery snow.

They came to a stop several feet from where I'd made my stand, their eyes flitting back and forth, scanning for Talia when they realized I was alone on the path. The leader of their group gave the order to attack and waved the others forward. They fanned out in a semicircle formation and moved in.

I shifted my weight, coiling my energy in my haunches and lunged at the demon on the far left. My claws pierced his thick hide and fangs clamped down on his neck. I shook my head back and forth until a large chunk of flesh ripped free.

He clamped his meaty hands around my sides and wrenched me loose, dragging my claws through his skin in the process. The demon dropped to his knees, blood pouring from his wounds and staining the ground around him, the black, viscous fluid a stark contrast to the stark white snow.

The others converged on me and that's when Talia made her move. She leapt out from behind the snow drift and tackled the demon in the back. They tumbled to the ground in a snarling heap of fur and leathery skin, each grappling for dominance over the other. Talia's small stature gave her the advantage. She was light, nimble and able to outmaneuver the demon, biting and clawing the demon each time she shifted position. His blood spilled onto the ground, pooling around his dead body.

Two down, two to go.

Talia and I closed ranks. The demons did the same. We faced off like opposing teams at the scrimmage line, each side waiting for the other to make the first move.

My lips curled back in a vicious snarl, showcasing my lethal fangs tinted black from the blood of their fallen brother-in-arms. I pawed at the ground, gouging claw marks deep into the snow, taunting them to attack.

Defense was the best offense. It was easier to spot and use their weaknesses against them when they made the first move.

Except they didn't.

The leader barked an order to the other demon in a language that sounded similar to Latin, turned and ran with his comrade hot on his heels.

"What just happened?" Talia sent her question through our mating bond, seemingly as baffled by their actions as I was.

"I have no idea." It was a first for me.

None of the demons we'd cross paths with before had backed down from a fight. They stood their ground, win or lose.

"They might be setting a trap. We should wait a little while before shifting in case they come back hoping to catch us without any weapons at our disposal. Are you hurt?" I padded around Talia, checking her for any wounds.

To my relief, the only blood that matted in her fur was black, not red.

"I'm okay. What about you? Are you hurt?" Talia circled around me, performing her own examination.

"Bruised ribs. They'll be fine once I shift back." I paced around the battleground, riding the adrenaline high while we waited for another attack.

But none came.

"What the hell? Why would they run?" I tried to make sense of the demons' retreat and each time came to one conclusion. "Unless someone called them off."

"The goddess?" Talia picked up on my line of thinking through the bond. "Do you think she sent them? But why call them off?"

"No, I don't think it was the goddess this time. I think your stalker sent a few of his minions to do what Darius failed to do, but he must have called them back before they could join their brethren." My logic was sound, although I wasn't entirely convinced.

Neither was Talia.

"I guess that makes sense, but..."

"I know. There was still a chance for his demons to capture

you. If one of them managed to land a couple good blows, break a leg or my jaw, the other could grab you and take off."

Talia shuddered as I described an alternate scenario to the one that had played out.

We let as much time as we could spare pass before shifting back and picking up the trail on our search for the demon wolf goddess. It didn't take long to find her.

Less than five miles into the second leg of our journey a wall of demon wolf acolytes formed in front of us, blocking off the path.

"Talia Linetti, Princess of the Bone Clan, your presence is required in the temple of the demon wolf goddess, Leto." A woman that I assumed to be the leader of the goddess's devotees stepped forward and pointed at a crevice in the side of the mountain with the tip of her sword. "The goddess expected you hours ago, and I assure you, she is not a patient being."

"We had a pack of demons on our tail and—"

"Save your excuses for Leto. They make no difference to me, and I don't care to hear them." She barked orders at the other devotees and pivoted on the heel of her leather sandal-clad foot.

The acolytes changed their line formation and closed in around us, like jailors escorting a dangerous and unpredictable criminal to her cell.

That did not bode well for our reception in the goddess' temple.

The leader's long, ebony braids swished over her shoulder when she walked away. The metal beadwork within them clanked against her armored bodice. Based on her movements and the command she had over the other women, it appeared they were more than devotees or acolytes serving in the goddess's temple.

They were her guards.

"We prefer the term shieldmaidens and I am Alita, their captain." She glanced back over her shoulder, full lips peeled back in a menacing smile that revealed sharp, oversized canines.

"How did you do that?" I asked, taken aback by her ability to see into my mind and read my thoughts.

Her intrusion caused a hitch in my step. One of the shield-maidens who'd taken up position behind me used the pommel of her sword to shove me forward.

"Do you think she can tap into our bond and eavesdrop on our conversations?" Talia used our connection and sent her question through the bond.

I waited a moment to see if Alita answered Talia's question the same way she had mine.

"She hasn't said anything. So it doesn't seem like she can access or mating bond," I wouldn't put it past the captain to pretend she couldn't hear what we said in the hopes of gleaning useful information for her goddess. It's what I would have done. "Or she doesn't want us to know that she can."

"We need to watch what we say and think from now on. If she can read minds then the goddess probably can too." Talia slipped her hand in mine and entwined our fingers together.

"It stands to reason, since she was able to send you those visions in your dreams." I glanced over at Talia, assessing the firm set of her jaw and hardened expression.

She gave my hand a reassuring squeeze and closed the connection from her side of the mating bond.

"You should take lessons from your friend, alpha." Alita advised, addressing me without as much as a backward glance. "She's putting up walls, locking everything down. But you? You think so loudly it's as if the words are coming out of your mouth."

Talia tilted her head in my direction and gave a curt nod, confirming what the captain had said. She'd figured out a way to block Alita's abilities or at least barricade her most private thoughts.

I imagined a safe in my mind, one with no visible locking mechanism or combination that only I could access. The thoughts and memories I held most dear or were of the greatest importance became files that I stored inside for safe keeping.

"Fast learner." Alita grunted what sounded akin to approval and marched on toward the widening crack in the rockface.

I couldn't help but wonder why she bothered to say anything to me at all about blocking her out, but erased the questions from my mind before I projected my thoughts.

"The temple is on the other side of the mountain. We go through here." Alita reached the crevice and pressed her palm against the side of the cracked stone.

"I don't see any rope or harnesses. Where's your climbing gear?" Talia glanced around, searching for any equipment that would help us on our ascent. "You don't expect us to free climb? Do you?"

There was a hint of apprehension in her voice, but she was quick to tamp it down before the shieldmaidens could take it as a sign of weakness and use it against her.

"I did not say over. I said through. Use your ears, princess. The goddess does not appreciate being made to repeat herself."

Alita closed her eyes and muttered something in another language.

The mountainside rumbled and shook as the crack in the rockface splintered open, expanding until it revealed a tunnel wide enough for a well-equipped demon army to pass through with ease.

That must have been where the demons that attacked us had come from and it stood to reason that there were more cracks between our worlds spread out all over the country. It was the central hub of the portal system the demons used to launch their attacks on the witches, my pack and others within the alliance.

"After you." Alita jerked her head toward the opening of the tunnel and fell in step behind us with the point of her sword aimed at my back.

Two of the acolytes waited for the portal to close once the entire party had passed through and took up positions on either side of the crevice from inside the mountain. A warm glow, the size of a lightning bug, expanded into a full flame as torches on the wall ignited and illuminated the tunnel.

Talia grabbed my hand; her palm clammy as she clutched it to hers. I was on edge too. We'd gone all in, risked it all - Talia's freedom, my pack, our future - to find the demon wolf goddess and plead for her help.

If the Goddess Leto refused, it had all been for nothing, and Talia and I were as good as dead.

The tunnel led us to an underground city with sand-packed roads, aquifers and stone bridges that arched over an inky black river that resembled demon blood. I almost asked Alita if it was, but thought better of it. Unless the goddess planned on forcing me to go for a swim, I didn't want to know the answer.

There were small homes, with terracotta tiled roofs and smooth clay walls. A bustling marketplace occupied the village square and high on a hill overlooking it all sat a massive temple carved out of glistening white marble, complete with Greek columns and statues that resembled the old gods of a long abandoned religion.

"This looks like something straight out of a history book." Talia's eyes widened as she took in the expansive city the goddess had created deep within the earth.

We were overdressed in our arctic gear for the warmer climate and shed a couple of layers of clothing to adjust our bodies to the mild temperature.

"Keep moving." Alita pushed ahead, assuming her position at the head of the group, and led us down the sandy streets and up the temple steps to Leto's temple.

The goddess sat on a marble throne, her dusky olive skin and ebony hair the only contrast to the stark white stone and silken robes that adorned her body.

"Ah, finally I can cast my gaze upon the princess who has captured the attention of my dear husband." Leto's venomous tone suggested the feelings she held for her husband were anything but affectionate. "A fair haired beauty, blessed with supple youth."

"Goddess, I must speak with you." Talia stepped forward, ready to plead her case at Leto's feet but the pointed glare of the demon wolf goddess stopped her in her tracks.

"You dare to enter my temple and make demands after all the trouble you've caused me, nymph?" Leto raised her hand to stay the guards who'd stepped into an offensive stance at her raised voice.

"Please, goddess. I didn't ask for this, any of it. I've never even seen your husband. I have absolutely no interest in marrying him or whatever else he's planning." Talia dropped to her knees and bowed her head, her blonde hair falling around her face like a golden curtain. "I already have a mate. I'm in love with Galen. You must have seen that when you came to me in my dreams. Please. You have to believe me."

"More demands." Leto leapt to her feet, silk pooling at her feet and cascading down the steps at the base of her throne. "How bold you are to assume that I have to do anything you say. Especially believe the lies that fall from your serpent tongue. You remind me of another temptress who collapsed, begging at the feet of a goddess. You would do well to hold your tongue before your physical likeness matches hers as well."

The goddess glided down the steps, stalked toward me and clamped her hand over my mouth before I had a chance to utter a word in Talia's defense.

"The mate, I presume?" Leto removed her hand and walked a circle as she sized me up. "The lover scorned by his betrothed's betrayal. You and I have much in common, Galen Long Claw."

"Talia hasn't betrayed me. She isn't like your husband." I spoke the truth but should have chosen my words more carefully and not drawn the goddess's ire.

"You defend her while she bears the mark of Lupercus?" Leto rounded on Talia, grabbed her by the wrist, dragged her to my feet and held her arm up for me to see the brand on Talia's skin. "You're weak, alpha. You disgust me. Remove them from my sight. A night in the chained in the dungeon's should free the truth from their mouths."

Our first encounter with the demon wolf goddess hadn't gone as we'd hoped. Still things could have gone worse. She hadn't killed us.

Yet.

# CHAPTER 6

# TALIA

Leto ordered Alita and the other shieldmaidens to take us from the temple and be thrown into separate prison cells below.

"Don't fight them." Galen reached out through our mating bond and explained why he'd chosen imprisonment over battling our way out of the temple. "She isn't through with us. No yet. We still have a chance to convince her to help us, but not if we fight."

I knew he was right. I'd come to the same conclusion and planned to suggest it before he communicated with me through our bond.

Still, that knowledge did little to quell my wolf's desire to fight her way out of the temple, past the acolytes that stood guard at the portal and back onto Alaska's frozen ground. She was tired of cells and chains, of being locked away for doing nothing but merely existing.

So was I.

But I followed Galen's advice, and my own judgment, and allowed myself to be taken into the goddess's custody.

Galen and my hands were bound behind our backs with iron shackles attached by a chain to a collar around our necks. Burlap sacks were draped over our heads before we were marched out of Leto's throne room and down into the catacombs below the temple.

Alita split her team of guard's in two. The first group had been assigned to Galen, while she and four other shield-maidens took charge of moving me into my accommodations for the night.

I couldn't see or hear Galen in the traditional sense. They made sure that we were placed in cells at opposite ends of the dungeon. But I knew that he was okay. I could feel him and talk with him through our bond. That had been enough to get me through the night.

We'd been right in assuming Leto wasn't finished with us.

Alita and her fellow acolytes hadn't laid a hand on us other than to place us in our cells. That was as far as their kindness went. The chains stayed on. Our collars were fastened to a bolt secured in the wall near the ceiling, forcing us to remain on our feet - or in my case on tiptoe - for the duration of our confinement.

It was another long night, with no food or water and no relief from the burning ache in my shoulders.

I'd lost sensation from my fingertips to my elbows due to the position of my arms twisted behind my back, hours before Alita returned and unlocked the door to my cell. She unhooked my collar from the wall mount, catching hold of the shackles around my wrists before I collapsed on the floor.

"Where's Galen? Is he all right?" I shifted my weight in her arms, turning so that I could look her in the eyes.

"Please, princess." Alita scoffed and shoved me toward the cell door. "There's no need to pretend you don't already know. Your ability to speak to Galen Long Claw through a mating bond is the only reason the two of you are still alive."

"I knew it." I cast a backward glance over my shoulder at the captain of the goddess's guards. "Galen did too. You weren't fooling anybody yesterday."

"You think you're clever, princess." Alita arched her brow and smirked. "We shall see just how clever you really are before the day is out."

Another group of guards marched down the hall with Galen, still bound and chained, behind them.

"It's okay. We're okay. We're still alive, right?" Galen reached out through the bond and locked his gaze with mine as he walked past. The goddess wants something from you or we'd be dead by now."

Alita made her presence known inside our connection for the first time, but I felt certain she'd been there from the moment she stepped into our path back on the hiking trail in the Gates of the Arctic.

"Enough." Her voice cut like a knife through our mating bond. "Silence from this moment on. You are prisoners in the house of the Goddess Leto. You will only speak when spoken too. With or without your precious bond."

She waited for the other group to take Galen upstairs, stepped out into the corridor, jerked on my chains as she led me back up to Leto's throne room.

Galen was seated on the steps at the base of Leto's throne

as if he were her pet. His chains had been removed but he was in now way free to leave. Whatever transpired between the goddess and Galen, I had no doubt it involved multiple threats on my life.

"There you are, little nymph. Have you come to speak the truth about the mark you bear on your arm and the blessed day of your union with my husband?" Leto phrased her question as if I had a choice in appearing before her.

"Goddess Leto, I told you the truth yesterday. These marks were forced upon me the same as his proposal. Galen is my chosen mate." I fought the urge to scream my innocence at the top of my lungs and checked my tone. Acting defensive was not the way to sway Leto to my side.

"Perhaps. Perhaps not." Leto ran her hands over her lap, smoothing the folds of her flowing gown. "I fear there is nothing that you can say that will convince me. Though I do admit an interest in the presence of a bond between you and the alpha."

"What can I do to prove to you that I am telling the truth?" I dipped my head and bent at the waist in a submissive pose as much as the chains that bound me would allow. "I came seeking your help and am at your mercy."

"That may be the first honest thing you have said since entering my temple." She clapped her hands twice and ordered Alita to remove my chains. "You are at my mercy."

Leto leaned back on her throne and crossed one leg over the other. She tapped her fingernails against the carved arms of the marble seat and pretended to contemplate my fate. We all knew it was a show. She'd made her decision about what she'd planned to do with me long before Galen and I arrived.

"I find myself in a generous mood today, princess. You wish to prove your innocence. I'm willing to allow it." Leto stood, looming over the throne room and the acolytes assembled inside it. "You will complete three trials. Your innocence will be determined by your success or failure in the challenges I set before you. Fail and you die. Your first trial starts now."

Alita drew her sword from its sheath and smacked it against her armored breastplate. The shieldmaidens answered with a thunderous clang of hardened steel blades colliding with their body armor.

Galen's hands clenched into fists at his side, but he made no attempt to get up from his place at the goddess's feet. Her hand fisted in his hair may have had something to do with it.

A seed of fear planted itself in my mind, threatening to grow wild and choke out my last shred of confidence. Alita was a seasoned warrior. Dressed and armed for battle. There were no rules of engagement, which meant I wasn't left defenseless.

I still had my wolf and the ability to shift.

But my fangs and claws were useless unless I could fight on the inside. Which meant I needed to get past the point of her sword. A feat easier said than done. If I succeeded, her armor posed yet another problem. Hard leather cuffs covered her forearms and matched the make of the boots laced up to her knees. Chainmail adorned her neck and draped down to her elbows, making her body all but impenetrable.

I was still sizing her up, searching for weak spots in her armor and stance, when the line of shieldmaidens changed position. They formed a ring, circling around me and Alita. The captain of the guard raised her sword above her head and shouted a battle cry loud enough to rattle the rafters and strike fear in the hearts of her enemies.

It sure as hell worked on me.

Anita dropped into a fighting stance with her arm drawn back and sword poised for driving its way through her opponent - me.

I called my wolf, tapping on the mating bond with Galen to borrow his strength and increase the speed of my transformation. She rushed forward, ripping through my skin before I'd stripped out of my clothes, and took control. Shredded cloth showered down and littered the floor around her paws like bits of confetti in a ticker tape parade.

She crouched down, coiling energy in her hind legs and made the first move. She pushed off and leapt across the makeshift ring. Alita saw her coming and adjusted her stance and drove her sword up in the air to spear my wolf as she came down.

There wasn't enough time to adjust course midair and miss Alita's sword entirely. My wolf rolled right, the razor sharp edge of the blade grazed our side. The captain of the goddess's guard drew first blood. My wolf fell to the floor, her white fur streaked red.

Alita returned to her defensive stance, ready for another attack. The fight was unfolding just as I feared, with the goddess's champion holding her position and waiting for me to attack, preventing me from getting on the inside. We hadn't found her weakness to exploit or any other way to gain the upper hand.

I couldn't lose. Not in the first of the goddess's trials - or the last.

One cut and a little blood wasn't enough to stop my wolf. She wanted to charge again but that wouldn't work. We couldn't defeat Alita that way. She'd carve us to pieces one slice of her sword at a time.

We needed to make her move, get her on the offensive to attack us instead. It sounded like a solid plan. There was just one problem. I had no idea how I was supposed to get her to do that.

Or how I was supposed to convince my wolf to go along with it.

Galen's energy flowed through our mating bond and settled my wolf. As an alpha he knew how to bring his wolves to heel, and I was one of his wolves. He asserted his dominance as pack leader over my wolf and helped me bring her back under my control instead of the other way around.

I stayed on my side of the ring, planted my paws on the ground, and dug in. If Alita wanted to defend her goddess's honor and the title of champion, she'd have to come to me to get it, but she held her ground. Alita stepped right. I stepped left. Neither of us moved forward.

We were at a stalemate.

Until the captain grew tired of waiting. She rushed forward and shifted before her paws hit the ground. I knew that Alita was a demon wolf, but what I hadn't known was that she was a demon dire wolf. She was at least twice my size, but my chances of success in my first trial increased ten fold.

My smaller size had been an advantage against other wolves. Dire wolf or not, I knew how to fight when both me and my opponent were on four legs. My lips curled back on a toothy growl and my claws were out.

I was under her belly when she landed, my nails gouging through the thinner coat and tender skin. Blood gushed from the wounds on her stomach. She slid across the floor, her paws scrambling for purchase on the slick marble, and crashed into the legs of one of the shieldmaidens forming the ring around us.

Alita got her paws back under her and pushed herself up off the floor. From the sound of her growl, it was clear she was seeing red - and not just from the blood I'd spilt. She came at me again, but her movements were slow, more pronounced, from the wound across her stomach.

I waited until I saw my opening, storing the energy I needed to make my move in my hind legs, and pounced. It was hard to hit a moving target. I'd been aiming for her neck, but connected with her shoulder. I bit down, locked my jaws and dug my claws in her side. She tried shaking me off, but I held on like my life depended on it.

Because it did.

As much as I needed, and I wanted to win the trial, I didn't want to kill Alita to do it. But the captain had too much fight in her for her own good and didn't know when to quit. She needed to learn when to stay down.

I had to be the one to teach her.

Alita dropped to the floor and rolled from left to right, still trying to knock me off her side. She'd done half the work for me by taking the fight to the ground. I scratched down on her shoulder, deepening the puncture wounds in her shoulder from my teeth, and jerked my head back until I took a piece of her with me.

She howled and rolled to her left, leaving her throat

exposed. That was the mistake that ended the fight. I moved in for the kill, biting her neck, but stopped short of finishing her.

The room fell silent. Everyone, Alita included, seemed to be waiting for me to rip her throat out.

I chose mercy in the hopes that Leto would do the same.

"Why have you stopped?" The demon wolf goddess shouted from her perch on the throne. "Do you wish to yield, princess? Because my champion will not."

Alita crawled to the edge of the ring, taking refuge at the feet of her shieldmaidens. She shifted to her human form and back again to heal her wounds.

"There, you see." Leto rose from her seat and ordered her captain to finish me off. "Victory was within your grasp and you threw it away."

But the demon wolf goddess had overestimated the captain of her guard.

Alita, her fur coated with tacky blood, padded across the floor, lowered her head and dropped into a submissive pose. The captain of the guard, Leto's champion, admitted defeat and yielded the fight.

I shifted, and stood before the demon wolf goddess in my human form, naked, exposed and completely vulnerable. If she had decided to go back on her word and kill me I would be helpless against her.

"It would seem you bested my champion." Leto stepped off her dais and crossed the throne room, stepping through the opening the shieldmaidens parted to provide for her. She hovered over her captain and it was clear by the look of disdain in her eyes that there would be repercussions for Alita's actions - or lack thereof.

"It would seem so, goddess." I bowed before her, low enough to expose my neck and waited for a blow that never came before standing at my full height.

Leto spun on her heel, the trail of her white satin gown sweeping over the floor behind her as she walked back to her throne. She stopped when she reached Galen, stooping to cup his face in her hands. She stroked her thumbs over his cheeks and then his lips before kneeling down and claiming his mouth in a kiss he didn't return.

Not that Galen's refusal seemed to bother her.

"My husband has claimed your mate. He will marry her and take her to his bed. His new bride and lover. Perhaps it's time that you and I did the same, alpha." She ran her tongue over his mouth, tracing the curve of his lips. "After all, it has been some time since I've felt the strength of a man's hands on this body. Don't worry princess, I have a voracious appetite but I promise to be gentle with him. There will be enough of your mate's libido left for when my husband grows tired of you. Though, Galen may have changed his mind about your future together by then."

Galen reached for me through our bond and pleaded with me not to take her bait. Leto wanted to goad me into a jealous rage. No doubt with the hopes that I would attack her, giving her the freedom to go back on her word and order my immediate execution.

My wolf railed against the sight of another woman laying hands on our mate. But I suspected Galen was right, as usual. He had an uncanny ability to read people and Leto seemed to be no exception, despite her elevated status as a goddess. She could have taken any number of lovers over the centuries but chose to remain faithful to her husband. She didn't want my mate, she wanted Lupercus, the demon wolf god she married.

"I hope you're ready for your next challenge, because this is all the respite you will have." Leto at least had the decency to order a change of clothes be brought to me before conjuring a portal and casting me through it. "The second trial begins now."

On the surface, the next task given to me by the demon wolf goddess seemed easier than defeating her strongest warrior. A game of lost and found. Recover Leto's most precious possession, taken by her husband in one of his vengeful moods and hidden in a location outside of realm and her reach.

But when I stepped through the portal and onto the other side, I realized what an impossible task it really was.

An arrowhead, formed out of obsidian that had once belonged to her daughter Artemis. The broken piece was all that remained of the arrow fired by the goddess of the hunt when she created the constellation Orion. Lupercus hid the arrowhead in a Foloi forest.

The second challenge felt more like a wild good chase in search of a needle in a haystack. But I couldn't return to her temple empty handed. I had to find the arrowhead. My life - and Galen's - depended on it.

CHAPTER 7

# GALEN

Talia was gone again. Except this time she hadn't been taken against her will. The demon wolf goddess started the second trial and sent her on a ridiculous treasure hunt for some precious arrowhead she'd lost hundreds of years ago.

I suspected the demon wolf goddess knew it was an impossible task and had set Talia up for failure. Which, of course, she denied when I accused her of doing as much.

"Galen, your harsh words wound me." She feigned distress, pressing her hand to her chest over the place where her heart would have been if she'd had one.

I knew her history, the life that she had before she adopted a new identity as the demon wolf god. As the mother of Artemis and Apollo, two important characters in werewolf lore, she was also an important part of our mythos. But Leto had become petty and cruel over the centuries since her tryst with

Zeus and subsequent banishment and years of torment by his wife, Hera.

It seemed even the fate of the gods was not without a sense of irony.

The demon wolf god married a philanderer not unlike her first lover and stepped into Hera's role as the bitter and cruel jilted wife. She was repeating the cycle but had been blinded by the pain of her husband's betrayal and couldn't see it.

"Walk with me, Galen." Leto held out her hand, expecting me to take it in mine and act as her escort. "Your mate will be gone quite a while on this next challenge, and I'd like to stretch my legs. Surely you must feel the same way. Besides, it will help you pass the time until the little nymph returns."

I considered pointing out her resemblance to stories I'd read in my youth about Hera but bit my tongue since I needed Leto to create another portal for Talia's return. There was no telling how the demon wolf god would react and couldn't afford to lose my temper and jeopardize Talia's safe return.

Leto grew impatient and grabbed my hand, pulling me from my seat on the marble steps. She crooked my arm at the elbow and looped hers through, resting her hand on my forearm.

"Tell me about your mate." She led us out of the temple and into an adjacent garden. "I admit to being curious about her. I can see how her fair hair and skin caught my husband's eye, but there must be something I've failed to see in her that has captured your attention as well."

"Talia is loyal, sometimes to a fault and her own detriment. She gives everyone the benefit of the doubt, again to her own detriment. She-"

"Sounds naive." Leto scoffed, slipping her arm from mine once we were safely inside the garden walls. "Even in my earliest memories I was not that innocent or simple minded."

"She's not simple minded." I'd had enough of Leto and her bullshit. "She's kind. You're just too cold hearted to know the difference."

"I think you might be more like my husband than I thought. Blinded by a pretty face." The demon wolf goddess teased, her voice and demeanor lighthearted for the first time since we'd arrived at her temple. "Or perhaps you want someone who does as they're told."

"It sounds like you're projecting. Talia is far from obedient." I chuckled at the thought. She's more my equal than any woman I've been in a relationship with before and if your husband thinks otherwise, he's lucky she wants nothing to do with him. Otherwise, he'd be in for a rude awakening."

"Perhaps I should send her to him then. It would serve him right." Leto smiled and it was easy to see why Zeus and Lupercus had fallen for her so many centuries ago.

Her mood shifted with the breeze, expression darkening as her thoughts turned back to Lupercus.

There were three endings to every love story - his, hers and the truth. It took two people to make or break a relationship, but Leto and Lupercus may have been the exception to that rule. From the outside looking in, it appeared that their love was toxic and dysfunctional from the start.

But the heart wants what the heart wants.

I doubted if there was anyone, mortal, wolf or demon that could have convinced Leto that she would be happier with someone who loved her the way she wanted to be loved. Talia and I were proof of that. Despite everything we'd been through, we found each other and formed a mating bond.

Ours was a love worth fighting for.

And Talia was still fighting for it. She'd gone through the portal in search of Leto's token alone. Whatever dangers she faced - and I knew there would be, because the demon wolf goddess wanted to punish Talia - she faced them on her own.

My wolf stirred, stalking his was out of the shadows of my soul and clawed at the barrier that separated our two natures. The longer she'd been gone, the more restless and agitated he became.

That made two of us.

"Am I boring you?" Leto's question and acidic tone pulled me out of my thoughts and back into the moment. "Maybe you'd find my husband better company. You have so much in common. I'm certain the conversation would be entertaining."

"I'm not interested in having a conversation with Lupercus. Unless my fists can do the talking. He'll have a hell of time getting me to shut up then."

My wolf perked up. He'd wanted to take the fight to the demon wolf god ever since we learned he was the one who'd marked Talia. Part of me - a massive part of me - agreed with him, but Talia had a plan and I'd promised to try things her way.

"Anger." Leto pinched a wilted bloom from a plant that I didn't recognize, examined the browned edges of the shriveled orange flower, and tossed it on the ground. "That is an emotion I am quite familiar with. I do long to feel other things. It has been so long since I've felt happiness. I would even welcome a bout of melancholy as respite from the hatred that has settled in the very fiber of my being. I believe this was the true punish-ment Hera intended for me."

I wasn't sure what she expected me to say - if anything - so I said nothing and just listened while she relived past tragedies.

I almost felt sorry for her. Almost. But when I thought of the demons she'd unleashed on the descendants of the Deofol pack and cities across the country, all the innocents were-wolves, witches and ordinary people who died just because Leto had a broken heart, I couldn't find an ounce of pity for her.

"Is that how you justify all of this?" I asked when I'd grown tired of indulging her sob story and couldn't hold my tongue any longer. "The demons you sent to do your dirty work, do you have any idea what they've been doing while you sit around and mope?"

"Do you take issue with the way I rule over my dominion?" Leto raised her hand, curled his fingers inward and squeezed them into a fist in front of my face.

The demon wolf goddess's power rose with her temper, and I learned first hand how she came by her name and exactly who fell under her dominion. Wolves and that included werewolves.

She commanded my wolf, ripped him from the dark corners of my mind and forced him to the surface. She brought on my transformation, the same way an alpha could with members of their pack. Instead of shortening the time or easing the pain of the change, she drew out the agonizing process, ensuring I felt every crack and pull of flesh and bone.

I collapsed at her feet, my fur slicked with blood and sweat, and tongue lolled out of the side of my mouth as I panted.

Everything hurt, from nose to tail. Even my canine teeth ached. It was worse than my first shift.

"You were saying?" Leto knelt in front of my, grabbed my muzzle and forced me to meet her gaze. She cocked her head to one side, listening to my whines and whimpers from the pain burning its way through my nerve endings. "I am Leto, goddess of demons...and wolves. This is but a taste of what I am capable of. You are a wolf, which makes you and your so called mate mine to do with as I please."

She released her physical hold on me but kept a tight reign on the metaphysical which controlled the shift and which nature - animal or man - was in charge of our body.

"Let's see how well you heel." Leto snapped her fingers and my wolf snapped to attention, pushing himself to his feet and standing at her side. When she moved, we moved. "I think I prefer your company this way."

He followed her around the garden and her commands to sit, stay, and heel, but he didn't like it. Neither did I.

If this was the way she treated her subjects, then she was unfit to rule. We'd come to her for help in our fight against Lupercus, the demon wolf god, but she was just as thoughtless and cruel as he was.

My wolf and I tried to break free of Leto's hold but she pumped more of her energy through our bodies, crushing us under the weight of her power. We reached for our bond with the pack but she'd severed the connection. I had no way to reach them, to let them know where I was and that their alpha was still alive, or tap into the pack's power.

The mating bond with Talia was still there and functional. I felt her energy at the end of the tether that connected us, but I couldn't reach out to her. Not without putting her at risk in the goddess's trials. I would not do anything to jeopardize her safety or her ability to win the challenge.

As much as I despised Leto, and hated to admit that we needed her help, the painful truth was that we did. We couldn't defeat all of the demons she'd unleashed and her husband on our own. We'd already tried that and it didn't work. We needed her help winning the battle ahead of us back home.

There was also the small problem with walking out of Leto's temple with our lives.

Talia had to succeed. She had to find the goddess's treasure, move on to the third trial and finish this once and for all.

I wouldn't be the reason she'd failed, and neither would my wolf.

We padded alongside the demon wolf goddess, winding our way down a pea gravel path through her garden to a small orchard filled with fruit trees, berry bushes, and a beehive. All the while struggling with our alpha instincts to fight for our independence.

My wolf and I were used to leading, not following. Even under my father's reign, we served in a position of authority before taking over responsibility of the pack. Obedience went against our very nature, but for Talia's sake we obeyed.

"I wonder how your mate is fairing in Foloi? Centaurs used to roam among those oaks until man encroached on their territory and all but wiped them out. Though it has reached my ears that the last remaining herd has been growing in number."

Leto reached down and ran her palm over the top of our head and scratched behind our ears, treating us like a domesticated house pet.

"They never were very fond of wolves. I do hope she doesn't cross paths with one. It would be a pity if something happened to her or the baby."

Baby? Was Talia pregnant or was Leto screwing with me? Talia hadn't said anything, but it could have been too early in the pregnancy for her to know. It was possible she didn't realize she was pregnant.

Were Talia and I really going to be parents? If so, it was just further proof that she was my true mate. There was no way anyone, not even a damned demon wolf god, could deny our bond.

But what if something happened to the baby? Talia would never forgive herself. If I knew my mate, she would sacrifice herself to protect our unborn child.

I was going to be a father. *A father.* I could hardly believe it. I'd wanted nothing more than to make Talia my mate and start a family together and had been making plans for our future almost from the moment I met her.

Still, I never expected that it would happen so soon, or in the middle of the nightmare we'd found ourselves in. There's never a perfect time, but our situation was less than ideal. What would Lupercus do if he found out that Talia had not only lost her virginity but carried my child inside her?

It was unlikely that he'd change his mind.

He'd set his sights on Talia and gone through a hell of a lot of trouble to not only claim her but bring her to his temple - wherever that was. We'd yet to find his location. Valerie was quick to give up information that led us to the goddess, but their god? Not so much.

At some point they abandoned worshiping Leto. Which

may have been another point of contention between her and her husband. He received all the accolades, the love and devotion of their followers that they once shared, while she'd been left with nothing. Not even the scraps of the demon wolves' affection.

I couldn't fix Leto's problems. Hell, I couldn't even fix my own without her help. The whole situation was a fucking mess.

Yet, somehow against all odds, Talia and I created life.

I wished my father would have been there to at least hear the news that the Long Claw pack would have a new heir or heiress to the throne. There had never been a female alpha in the history of our pack, but there was a first time for everything.

My heart thumped, swelling with pride over the news. News I'd yet to confirm with Talia, but somehow I knew that Leto spoke the truth.

She may have let Talia's pregnancy slip, but I suspected she'd done it to instill fear, to push my alpha wolf over the edge with the hopes that I would do something rash, something stupid that would cause Talia to forfeit.

From whom, or how I'd found out didn't matter. I was going to be a dad. My strong, beautiful mate had given me the greatest gift anyone could ever give.

If Talia gave birth to a baby girl, she'd grow up to be just like her mother. She wouldn't be just another pretty face. Our daughter would have the strength, wisdom and patience to lead - just like her mother.

Of course, if our baby is a boy, he would follow in his father's footsteps. The same way I had followed in mine and my father in his. All the way down the line to the first Long Claw and the founding of our pack.

That is, assuming we all survived.

I wasn't one to just assume anything. The old adage about making assumptions often proved to be true. So, I preferred to deal in facts. Something that we'd been lacking since the onset of this whole thing.

We'd been in the dark since the demons first arrived on our side to the barrier between the god and goddess's world and ours.

It was high time we turned on the light and kicked some demon ass.

Starting with Leto.

# CHAPTER 8
## TALIA

Searching for an ancient obsidian arrowhead in a dense forest of old oaks was no easy feat. Adding the centaurs and dryads that called the woodland home made it all but impossible. They hated wolves. All wolves - even half breeds like shifters.

I would have pointed out the irony in that, given their own dual natures, if I'd have thought they would have stopped to listen before trying to rid their forest of me.

Avoiding the woodland creatures had slowed me down. I spent more time hiding from them than I did looking for the damned arrowhead. At the rate I'd been going, I would be forced to forfeit the challenge.

Leto hadn't set a time limit on the second trial, but I seriously doubted it was infinite. She would put an end to my search and make a declaration that I had lost the challenge.

And my life.

It didn't make sense that the demon wolf goddess blamed

me for her husband's misdeeds. But nothing about our situation made sense. Especially, not the demon wolf god's infatuation with me or the pact between him and his devotees - the Deofol pack.

Their relationship seemed awfully one sided to me. He got the pick of their women, and they got what in return? Territory in Alaska? I assumed it was for the oil rights and the money and power that went along with it.

Because it sure as hell couldn't have been for the weather.

If my calculations were correct, I'd spent the better part of half an hour crouched behind a pile of decomposing, moss and mushroom covered wood. My hamstrings and calves were cramped. If my hiding spot were discovered by a centaur or a dryad, the knots in my legs would stop me before either of them could.

Another herd of centaurs galloped past. Once the last of them cleared my line of sight I made the decision to break from my hiding spot and continue my search for the lost arrowhead. I pressed my hand to the ground, checking for any vibrations from thundering hooves in the distance, and dashed out from behind the pile of rotted tree limbs.

I made it across a clearing in the forest to another cluster of trees and scurried around to hide myself behind the thick trunk. So far so good. I'd been lucky enough to avoid capture - there was a first time for everything.

If only that luck continued.

A dryad dropped down from her perch in a fork in the branches above me. She'd been so quiet and still, her natural coloring the perfect camouflage to disappear in the leafy canopy. She even smelled like the forest, making her undetectable to my heightened senses. The dryad caught me off guard and had me at a disadvantage.

"What business does a wolf have in Foloi?" She palmed a small blade, aimed for my face and prepared to throw the knife. "Wolves are forbidden in this forest."

"Leto sent me to-"

"The demon wolf goddess?" The dryad scoffed, bitter laughter bubbling up from a place of darkness within her. "Carrying Leto's banner won't win you any favors here, wolf."

"She's no ally of mine." *At least not yet.* I still needed her help, but the dryad didn't need to know that. I eased my hands up in the air, palms out, in a placating gesture. "Leto sent me here as part of a series of trials to prove my innocence. I have to find Artemis's obsidian arrowhead. If I don't find it and bring it back to her temple before the challenge ends, she'll end me. Though, I'm starting to think she might have sent me here for you to do that for her."

"None here will do Leto's bidding." The dryad lowered her arm and slipped the knife into a small sheath strapped to her upper thigh. "If the demon wolf goddess wants to see you dead, then you may have safe passage to complete your challenge. Find Artemis's arrowhead and leave Folios before the sunsets or you'll be forced to stay in the forest."

Forever.

She hadn't said it aloud, but it was implied. More threats. More promises. No matter what I did, the threat of death loomed over me.

"I don't suppose you know where it is?" I glanced around the forest, unsure of my surroundings or which direction to continue my search. "Or maybe you could give me a general heading? You know, a clue or something?"

Time moved at a different pace in the mythical forest than it did back home. Rainbow sherbet hues of raspberry pink, orange and lemon yellow streaked the sky. The sun was already going down. I was almost out of time and my trial had barely begun.

The dryad crossed her arms over her chest, crushing the bright green leaves and soft pink dogwood blossoms that made up the bodice of her flowing gown, and cocked her head to one side while sizing me up. She seemed to be contemplating my question, as if she had information but wasn't sure if she should share it.

"A victory for you would be a substantial loss for the demon wolf goddess?" The dryad mulled it over another for another minute or two after I nodded my answer. She scrunched her nose and made a face like she'd caught a pungent scent in the air - like mine. "And it will keep the forest free from creatures born into her domain."

"The less time I spend searching for the arrowhead, the less time I spend in your forest." I clasped my hands together and clamped down on my eagerness for her help - for anyone's help.

I was worried that if she realized what a boon her help would be for me, she might require something in return. My plate was full to overflowing. I couldn't heap an outstanding debt to a mythical creature on top of it.

Ridding the forest of a demon wolf seemed to be the real motivating factor in her decision. Any pain and suffering she caused Leto would have been a bonus.

"Artemis used to hunt these woods. She and Orion spent many nights together under the stars. Before she killed him, that is." The dryad relaxed her posture and motioned for me to follow her. "The arrowhead that pierced his heart is the very one you seek."

She led me through the forest, weaving a path through the trees to a small glen that opened up into a larger pasture on the left side.

"The elders say there was nothing special about the arrows in Artemis's quiver. She was the goddess of hunting and her skill was more than enough. It turned to blackened glass when she pulled it from Orion's chest. They say she buried it here, with her love for him."

"Here?" My gaze dropped to our feet and the spot in the ankle deep grass where we were standing. "Like, literally right here or here as in this general vicinity?"

From the dryad's pointed glare I surmised that I wouldn't be an x marking the spot out in the glen where Artemis had buried the arrowhead. If she had buried the arrowhead.

Leto made it sound as if it had once been in her possession and that at some point over ages she'd lost it. Of course, it seemed that the years hadn't been kind to the demon wolf goddess and she was a touch insane.

I had nothing to lose by digging in the field but time. Unfortunately for me, time was the one thing I couldn't afford to spare.

For whatever reason - probably because she didn't come off as a raging, jealous lunatic - I believed the dryad's story of the arrow more than Leto's.

I closed my eyes, pictured the pasture in my mind and

focused on the arrowhead. If it were me, if I was in Artemis's shoes and it had been my arrow that had killed Galen, where would I bury it?

The answer struck me like a bolt of lightning. I tilted my head back, glanced up at the pastel colored sky, and tried my best to accurately calculate the position of Orion's constellation. When I felt confident that I reached the correct location, I went out into the pasture and ripped the grass from the ground, roots and all.

I stripped down, called my wolf and let the shift rip through me. The dig went much faster with two paws and a whole lot of claws. My wolf and I tore through the dirt, widening and deepening the hole until we found what we were looking for.

The black arrowhead with its mirror-like surface and razor sharp edges, protruded from the bottom of the hole that I'd dug.

I couldn't believe that I had actually found the arrowhead. It was an educated guess, but a guess nonetheless and a huge part of me hadn't expected it to pay off. I thought I would have been digging long past sunset until I was trapped in the forest for good.

"The sun is almost gone. Grab your prize and go wolf." The dryad seemed equally pleased. No doubt because it meant that I would not be trapped in the forest.

I shoved my muzzle into the hole, and plucked the arrowhead from its hiding place and held it in my mouth taking care not to cut the inside of my cheeks with the sharp edges. Not bothering to waste time shifting back to my mortal form, I yipped  my thanks to the dryad and ran off the field, back the way we came through the woods to the portal that Leto had created.

The arrowhead worked as a key and activated the portal, opening it wide enough for me to pass through. My wolf struggled with the magic working to transport us from one place to another. It felt wild and dangerous to her - an unknown. We fought the urge to run the opposite direction of the pull of Leto's portal and popped back out inside the throne room of her temple.

I padded across the marble floor, up the dais steps to the base of the throne and spat the arrowhead out at Leto's feet.

Galen darted across the dais from his position seated on the floor in front of the demon wolf goddess and nudged me with his muzzle. He licked my face before walking a circle around me and examined me for wounds.

I felt his relief through our mating bond when he'd completed his once over and confirmed for himself that I was okay.

"I was so worried." Galen's emotions - all the anxiety and fear he felt of my well-being combined with the love he felt for me - blew the bond wide open.

The force of it all overwhelmed me and knocked me back a step, but I welcomed the emotional onslaught.

"I'm happy to see you too." I licked his muzzle and nuzzled against his neck, burrowing into his fur and drawing in his scent.

We curled up beside each other, spooning my back to his front at the bottom of the stairs and waited for Leto's confirmation that I had found the arrowhead and completed the trial.

I tamped down the fear and distrust of anyone outside the

Long Claw pack and listened as Leto retold the story of her son's betrayal of his sister, tricking her into killing her lover. The demon wolf goddess's version was similar to the dryad's - if not a little sadder. Whatever she felt for the gods who wronged her, for her husband or the wolves under her domain, she loved her children.

Her gratitude to have the arrowhead felt genuine. It was hard to reconcile a loving mother with the woman peering down at us. She hadn't exactly given off motherly vibes. Still, I hoped against hope that she would extend her appreciation by canceling the next trial.

Those hopes were dashed when Leto ordered that I be prepared for the third and final challenge at sunrise.

Her acolytes came in with wood for a small fire, bundles of freshly cut herbs that I wasn't able to identify and a black metal tea kettle. One of them set about stacking the wood for the fire, while another prepared the herbs and a third carried the tea kettle to fill with water from the creek that flowed through her garden.

"You need to get some rest tonight." Galen's voice caressed my mind the way his hands would have caressed my body if we were alone.

"I'm not tired." Rest was the last thing I thought about I was addicted to his touch, to him, and craved both the way a junkie craved their next fix. The look in his wolf's eyes said they felt the same way.

Frustration bubbled between us, flowing through both ends of the bond over our inability to do anything about it.

"Talia, there's something you need to know." His gaze

flicked to the demon wolf goddess's devotees." And you need to hear it before you start the next challenge."

His sudden shift in mood was concerning. I tracked his line of sight to the women working by the fire. Whatever happened while I was in Folios kicked his overprotective nature into hyperdrive.

"You're going to make yourself sick with worry, Galen. Just tell me what it is." My heart rate increased. The nervousness he projected through the bond began to rub off on me.

"While you were searching for the arrowhead, Leto told me…" He was focused on the devotees and whatever concoction they were preparing.

"Leto told you…" I prodded, and gave him a gentle nudge in the side with my nose.

"You're pregnant. A few weeks along. Still in the first trimester." Excitement churned into the mix of nervousness he emitted through our connection.

Which went a long way to ease the fear that his nerves were due to a negative reaction to Leto's news. I shouldn't have doubted him, however briefly. Galen wanted a family as much as I did.

"I thought so." My front paws curved toward my belly on instinct. There were no physical signs yet, but it wouldn't take long before there was a noticeable swell to my stomach. "Well, I hoped so, anyway."

"Why didn't you say anything?" Galen's tongue lolled out of his mouth, his joy resonating through the bond.

I pictured the curve of his lips, the way his mouth upturned at the left corner and produced a dimple in his cheek, and couldn't wait to continue this experience with him in our human forms. Our wolves rejoiced, and curled closer together. Their pride and happiness over growing their pack felt wonderful but I was greedy and wanted more, like feeling his fingers splayed and hand resting on my belly.

"It was while I was trapped in the cave with Darius. When our bond was still malfunctioning, I felt something else, another energy. It was faint. It felt like you but it wasn't you. There were pieces of me there too. So I thought there was a chance, but-"

"But with everything going on you were afraid that if you were pregnant and Lupercus found out he might do something to hurt the baby or use our child as leverage to manipulate you." Galen gave voice to the fears seeping out of the dark corners in my mind. "I thought the same thing when Leto told me, but I'm not going to let either of them ruin this. We're going to have a baby, Talia. A piece of me and you out there in the world. A future for the Long Claw pack."

I wasn't sure what I'd done to deserve having Galen as my mate but I planned to give thanks to the universe every day for bringing him into my life.

Any thought of giving up or giving in were wiped from my mind the second Galen confirmed my suspicions about our baby. If things weren't going the way we'd planned, I would have considered bargaining with Leto and Lupercus to keep my mate safe.

But the life we created together, our future, meant there would be no negotiations. I wanted a family and I would do whatever it took to keep Galen and our baby safe.

# CHAPTER 9

# GALEN.

Talia and I spent the night curled up in our wolf forms inside Leto's temple, curled up together at the base of the stairs that led up to her throne. I wanted to hold her in my arms, but we'd decided that until we could get her back home with access to medical care, it would be best if she limited her shifts.

Neither of us had personal experience with prenatal care and while pack magic infused in our DNA controlled our transformations, shifting was just as much a physical experience as it was a magical one. The manipulations and rearrangement of muscle, skin and bone applied to our developing baby as much as it did the two of us.

I uncurled myself from behind Talia and stretched my legs. It had been a long time since I'd spent so many consecutive hours and even slept through the night as a wolf, but I promised Talia that I would try to stay on the same schedule and rotation as her shifts whenever possible.

My wolf certainly hadn't complained.

The fire had burned down from a small campfire to a bed of smoldering coals. Steam billowed from the neck of the kettle that hung from a frame pitched over the fire pit, but there was no one to tend the flames of the brew that had been cooking over them.

Leto and her acolytes had disappeared at some time during the wee hours of the night.

I used my nose to nudge Talia in her ribs with my nose to wake her up. We were both exhausted but she needed the rest more than I did. Still, as much as I hated to wake her, it needed to be done. We had to see if we could figure out who - besides the demon wolf goddess - would want to hurt us.

It was a long shot that anyone would get the drop on the demon wolf goddess or her devotees, but with a baby on the way, Talia and I weren't taking any chances.

The list was longer than I would have liked. There were plenty of wolves in both the Northwood and Deofol packs that wanted to see Talia dead. We needed to watch our backs, but I doubted anyone had gotten the drop on Leto.

Not long after we'd compiled our list of possible suspects, one of Leto's devotees returned to her place at the fire ring and tended to the kettle. She removed it from the frame and poured it into a small clay mug.

I suspected that the demon wolf goddess would enjoy our suffering and want to be there to experience it for herself, but she was still missing in action when the devotee carried the clay mug over, set it in front of Talia and tried to wake my mate.

Talia stirred. The devotee was successful on her third attempt, but had gotten more than she bargained for. Talia pounced, knocking the acolyte to the ground and pinned the devotee beneath her.

"Goddess Leto sent me to you with specific orders for you to drink a cup of the tea that my sisters and I brewed." She cowered beneath Talia and pointed to the earthen ware at Talia's feet and mimed taking a drink. "Please princess, don't kill me."

The acolyte's reaction spoke volumes about the way that Leto ruled over her domain and treated those who worshiped at her feet. It seemed the demon wolf god was cruel whether you mistreated her or not.

Not that it came as a surprise. I'd suspected as much.

Talia swatted the cup away with her paw and sat back on her haunches, using her body weight to hold the woman in place. She seemed to be waiting for the acolyte to give her a reason to attack.

But the devotee must have learned her place in the pecking order the hard way because she remained still, not wanting to provoke Talia.

They were at a stalemate, with neither of them making a move to push the other into a fight.

I never wanted to see a look of fear in the eyes of any wolf in my pack like that of the woman pinned beneath Talia. That wasn't how I ran my pack, and neither had my father.

Talia's eyes had been opened to a different way of pack life when she joined the Long Claw pack. She'd been raised under an alpha who kept a choke hold on his wolves and ruled with an iron fist for personal gain and not the well being of his pack. An alpha who killed her father in cold blood.

But that wasn't an alpha's purpose. An alpha was a leader, not a dictator.

From what I'd seen, Leto and the Northwood alpha had a lot in common. Hell, she may not have wanted to admit it, since he is loyal to her husband, but she had an awful lot in common with Bjorn.

"Princess, please. The tea is for the final trial." The acolyte pleaded for mercy and for Talia to let her go. "I'm not here to hurt you. I'm just serving the tea, as I was told to do."

"Talia." I reached out to her through our bond, to calm her down and soothe her agitated wolf. "It's all right, sweetheart. She isn't going to hurt you or the baby."

"The tea could be poisonous." Talia snarled, hackles raised.

By that time, she would have already been skittish of wolves outside our pack. It was in their nature. Something ingrained in a mother's DNA. Talia and her wolf would do whatever they felt necessary to keep themselves and our unborn child safe.

Leto glided into the room. The lightweight fabric of her flowy gown swept the marble floor tiles behind her. She clasped her hands together and slowly clapped as she crossed the throne room.

"I dare say the two of you would make wonderful guard dogs." She stopped clapping, gripped the hem of her dress, and hiked it up above her leather sandals as she made her way up the steps to her throne. "Like Remus and Romulus. Refuse the third trial, nymph. I won't kill you. Stay here in your natural form and keep watch over my throne. I give you my word."

Talia sniffed the air and sneezed, like she'd caught a whiff of something she didn't like. It was the closest thing to an answer that the goddess was going to get.

"I suppose that is a no." Leto adjusted her gown and sat on the throne with one leg crossed over the other. She leaned back with a dramatic sigh, as if she had grown bored of Talia and the trials. "Then drink the tea, princess, and let's get this over with."

The goddess snapped her fingers and the acolyte bucked Talia off and scrambled to her feet. She scooped the clay cup off the floor and rushed to the kettle to refill it with the steaming liquid.

"You may want to shift back to your lesser form for this trial." Leto sighed and stretched her arms above her head, letting them fall dramatically back down at her sides. "Your greatest strength will be your weakness in this challenge."

Talia shifted her gaze from Leto to me, asking for guidance through our bond. She wanted to hear my thoughts before making her decision. Not to stay as wolves in Leto's court. She didn't need to ask how I felt about that, but in trusting Leto's advice about the last challenge.

If our places were reversed, would I have taken the demon wolf goddess's suggestion to change back to a human for the last trial? Especially considering her condition and the health of the baby.

Talia's wolf retreated when I gave her my answer. I felt the power shift between them and the wolf ease back into the recesses of Talia's soul as my mate stepped back out into the front. Her change had always been quick for a non-alpha were-wolf, but Talia slowed it down to an agonizing crawl.

I stayed with her, connected through our bond and felt

every joint point, bone shift, muscle stretch, as her body realigned and reformed itself into a human woman. It was only a fraction of the pain Talia experienced during the shift, but she wanted to be sure the transformation wouldn't damage our baby and I wanted to be there with her.

I planned to experience as much of this pregnancy as I could with her, sharing the highs and lows, easing her pain when I could, through our bond.

The acolyte slowed her pace on the return trip after refilling the cup from the kettle with fresh tea, taking care not to spill a single drop of the marble tiles. She handed the tea to Talia, who accepted the clay cup with a soft smile and offer of thanks.

"Drink it all, down to the last drop." Leto rested her elbows on her knees and propped her head in her hands. Her posture was casual, almost aloof, but I caught the flicker of interest in her eye.

I wasn't a witch and hadn't recognized any of the herbs that the devotees had used to prepare the tea. I thought I smelled liquorice or anise while they steeped the brew, but I couldn't be sure. What I did know was that whatever was in the kettle was no ordinary tea.

And the demon goddess seemed very interested in Talia's reaction to it.

One again my mate was about to descend on a journey of her own. Somewhere I couldn't follow and would be unable to protect her or our baby. I had to put my trust in Talia to keep herself and our child safe.

And I had every confidence that she would.

But knowing that Talia didn't need my help, that she was more than capable and would do everything and anything to prevent any harm from coming to them, didn't make it any easier to let her go somewhere that I couldn't.

"The tea is a strong psychedelic used by wolf pack medicine men and midwives for centuries. It thins the barriers between this world and the next, between conscious and subconscious." Leto steepled her fingers in front of her face and tapped the side of her index fingers against her lips. "Ready or not, princess, your trial is about to begin."

Talia's eyelids fluttered, then drifted shut. She rocked on her feet, swaying left and right like a drunken sailor on rough seas.

Leto eased back into her throne, draped her legs over the side of the chair and snapped her fingers. Three acolytes rushed across the room in response to her summons. I'd assumed they were there at her beck and call to answer to her every whim. But the women moved over to Talia, one on each side and the third at her back, and eased her down onto the floor.

The courtesy caught me off guard. Perhaps there was a sliver of Leto's humanity left and she wasn't entirely irredeemable.

Talia laid on her backside, her naked body arched toward the ceiling, writhing in pain. Her arms flailed above her head as if she was swatting at some invisible assailant. She spoke through her moans and cries of pain, but the words were undecipherable and I couldn't understand what she was trying to tell me.

It was unbearable to watch Talia suffer without any way for me to stop it or at the very least, console her but I forced myself not to look away. It was the only thing I knew to do. I couldn't fix it, couldn't take her pain and make it mine so that she never had to feel any of it, but I could stand witness for her.

Talia groaned, grimaced and clenched her teeth. A sheen of sweat coated her skin, but she was racked with chills. She curled into the fetal position, tucking her knees into her chest, and wrapped her arms around her legs.

I reached out through the bond but our connection was muddied by all of the emotional energy she pushed through the tie that bound us together. It felt like wading chest deep against the current in a storm surge. Whenever I gained an inch, moving closer to the center of our bond and reaching Talia, I was pushed back by another wave of her emotions.

"You can't help her." A soft, feminine voice whispered in my ear. "There's nothing you can do for her."

"She's in so much pain and you're helpless you stop it." Another voice came from behind me, but I refused to pull my gaze from Talia and turn around.

"The princess will blame you for this. Everything that is happening to her right now is because of you. If it wasn't for you, she would have given up, given in. She wouldn't be suffering right now. She's only doing this for you. Not because she wants to but because she thinks you want her to." A third voice whispered on my left.

They seemed to be reading my mind, giving voice to the dark thoughts tormenting me. They wanted me to break, to look away. To leave Talia.

That was Leto's back up plan. If Talia survived the trial, and beat the goddess at her own game, she wanted to have another way to make Talia suffer the same way the goddess had.

But I wouldn't give in.

The goddess wanted to break me, but her ploys had the opposite effect. She made me stronger, solidified my resolve to stand by my mate.

I was there when Talia started the challenge and I was damn sure going to be there when she ended it, cheering her on at the finish line.

Because she was going to win the challenge and we were going to walk out of there as a family. The goddess was going to keep her word.

Or I would make her regret it.

# CHAPTER 10

# TALIA

I stood in my father's house, suitcase packed and waiting for me by the front door. My car had been back up the drive and the trunk was open, waiting for me to shove the last of my belongings inside.

The scene felt familiar - because it was.

Familiar but not exactly how I remembered it or how I'd experienced it. Nyssa and Celia weren't there to help me pack and get out of town before Maddox and his father made good on their promise to kill me.

My father's cologne. The woodsy scent with citrus undertones wafted out from the living room, tugging at my heart strings and filling my mind with memories. Especially the time I saw him, witnessing his execution.

"Talia, is that you?" His raspy voice was music to my ears.

My legs threatened to give out on me, buckling at my knees. I grabbed the door jamb for support, and kept myself upright.

"Daddy?" My voice was soft, barely a whisper, but I knew he heard me.

"What are you doing here?" The arms of his favorite chair creaked under his weight as he pushed himself up.

I didn't need to be in the same room with him to know that's what made those sounds. I'd seen him get in and out of that old recliner too many times to count. It had been my father and I in that old house my entire life. I knew every creek, every crack, the house made and my father's schedule by heart.

I pried my fingers from the doorjamb and turned toward the sound of his voice. I couldn't believe I'd been granted another chance to see my father or that Leto had been the one to provide it.

Part of me wanted to know how Leto had managed to resurrect my father. The other part didn't care and didn't want to look at the magic too hard or ask too many questions for fear the spell would unravel and I'd lose him all over again.

"Didn't I tell you to pack your shit and go? Why are you still hanging around here, huh? You know if Maddox and his father see you here I'm a dead man." My father stumbled into the small foyer, reeking of cheap beer and stale cigars.

It had been a long time since I'd seen him this way. He'd gone on a few benders when I was little. He'd come home from the bar drunk and mean, saying hateful things but he never hit me and he always apologized in the morning.

It didn't make it right, but my father was a broken man after mother died. He did the best he could and I loved him.

"Daddy, they didn't come here looking for me. They came for you after the raid on the Long Claw pack. Something happened, and things didn't go according to plan." I summarized the events that lead up to his death, hoping it would jog his memory but he continued to lay the blame for his death at my feet.

And my mother's.

"I never should have brought her home. Things would have been different if I didn't marry her." He'd said that before and to some extent I think he meant it. But never where I was concerned.

His regret was never about me. It was the pain he suffered after she was gone.

"Your mother ruined everything. Even her daughter. Look at you, demons. The both of you. Tainted from the start and you both left an evil mark on me and my life. Ruined everything."

This wasn't my father. It couldn't be. He'd placed my mother on a pedestal the moment he met her.

"Dad?" I inched my way across the foyer, closing the distance between us. "I love you and I miss you so much."

I pulled him into a hug, wrapping my arms around him one last time. Something I'd wanted to do a million times since he was murdered by my former alpha.

But he didn't hug me back.

He just spewed the same venomous, hateful words over and over again, blaming me for his death - and the death of my mother.

The last one all but broke me. When I was a little girl all my birthday wishes had been the same. I wanted my mother to be with me and my dad.

"She would still be alive if it wasn't for you. Everyone dies around you, Talia. The cost of loving you is a high price to pay and it's not worth it. I'd trade a thousand of you on the exotic animal trader market for one of her."

I grabbed the door knob, turned and yanked it open, stumbling out of my childhood home and into the streets I used to run when I was a teenager. The same streets where I'd met and fallen in love with Maddox.

Where he was waiting for me like he had every day before school.

"Talia?" Maddox pulled his long hair back in a low ponytail, twisting it into a knot at the nape of his neck.

He wore the same letterman's jacket from high school, but there were fine lines around the corners of his mouth and eyes that aged him beyond his senior year.

I rushed out to the street to meet him. I needed to be held, to have my mates arms around me, holding me tight and telling me everything was going to be okay. Maddox filled that role for years and while my heart wanted Galen, my memory brought me back here.

"Whoa, what are you doing?" Maddox thrust his hand on, pressing the flat of his palm against the center of my chest and held me at arm's length. "In what world would the son of an alpha go out with a broke ass bitch like you? Even if your family had money or power, you'd still be a freak."

"Maddox, we were together for years, you said you loved me. You said you were my mate. You asked me to marry you." I didn't want the life that Maddox had planned for us anymore. Deep down, I'm not sure that I ever did, but this alternate version of my life had me out of sorts and out of touch with myself.

"Marry you?" Maddox laughed in my face. The rejection

stung even though I wasn't in love with him any more. "And risk having freak kids like you? You're crazy if you think I would want to taint my bloodline with the likes of you. Imagine a bunch of red eyed, demon wolf freaks running around claiming they're alphas. Bastards is more like it. I'd never admit they were mine. There is no way in hell I'd sleep with you. Never mind, knock you up."

Maddox clipped me with his shoulder and shoved me back. I wasn't prepared for the amount of force he'd put behind it. My feet weren't planted firmly beneath me, causing me to stumble backward. I lost my footing altogether and landed on my backside. The impact vibrated up my tailbone and rattled my teeth.

"Maddox, wait. I don't understand what's happening." I pushed to my feet, rubbing the ache in my lower back, but he was gone.

I was left there alone in the middle of the street, my jeans stained with road grime, socks and shoes soaked through from the puddle I'd stepped in.

The curtain in the front room window of the house I'd grown up in swished closed. My father watched the exchange from the living room and never bothered to come outside to my defense. He let Maddox insult me, hurt me and cast me aside like I was nothing. He didn't rip open the door and give my ex fiancé a piece of his mind. He just stood there and watched from behind the lace curtain.

Galen walked out from between the two neighboring houses. He didn't rush to my side the way he normally did, but moved at a slow calculated pace until he stood in front of me.

Less than an inch apart. The warmth of his breath settled across my face and I took comfort in his proximity.

I'd missed him, but it didn't seem the feeling was mutual.

He didn't say anything or reach for me in any way, He just stood there, staring at me like I was the freak that Maddox said I was.

I reached for Galen through the bond but it wasn't there. No, that wasn't exactly true. The bond was still there, but it wasn't accessible to me. It had been blocked off from Galen's side. Completely shut down .

Galen had closed himself off to me.

"Do you know how many of my pack died because of you? How many witches." His hands trembled as he curled them into fists at his sides. "My father. All of them died because of you. My father, Talia."

He screamed the last. His spittle landed on my chin and cheek. Galen pressed his forehead to mine, pushing bone against bone until I backed away from him.

"I didn't mean for any of this to happen. I didn't ask for this." I reached for him, to touch his face, cupping his cheek with my hand the way I'd done a thousand times since we fell in love.

"Well, it happened anyway. Because of you." Galen smacked my hand away. "You're expelled from the Long Claw pack. I revoke your membership and reject our bond."

"Galen, you don't mean that." I grabbed a hold of his shirt and tried to pull him into my arms. "Please, I love you and you love me. We're going to have a baby together, start a family. Please, please don't do this."

"I had a family. The greatest man, the greatest alpha, I'd

ever known and I buried him because of you and the demon wolves." The anger in Galen's eyes shattered my heart into a million pieces. "They're your real family, Bone Princess. Why don't you go home, beg Bjorn's forgiveness and rejoin the pack you should have been born into."

His words felt like a slap to the face, turning his back on me felt like a sucker punch to the solar plexus.

But the worst part was, everything that my father, Maddox, and Galen had said I'd heard before. Their words mirrored my darkest thoughts. The worst of what they said barely scratched the surface of what I'd thought about myself.

I didn't deserve Galen or a family. Everything and everyone that I came into contact with was ruined. Even Maddox had been sweet and loving when we started dating, but the longer we were together the more things changed. Until he and his father kicked me out of the Northwood pack.

I lost a father and so did Galen. The blame for both of those deaths could be laid at my feet. Galen was right. I should have stayed with the Deofol pack, joined the Bone Clan and accepted my place among them.

The demon wolf god was the only one who wanted me, despite the fact that I wanted nothing to do with him.

Should I have let him love me? Would that have washed the blood from my hands and saved countless lives? Was it my rejection of Lupercus that caused all of this? Would Max still be alive? And what about my father? Would the Northwood pack have still killed him?

I carried the weight of those questions in my mind while I searched for the exit of the nightmare that I seemed to be trapped in. I walked around the perimeter, testing the boundaries for weak spots or a way out, but couldn't find anything.

There was nothing left but me and my self-loathing.

My childhood home was gone. Dead grass and patches of dirt and the outline of the house's foundation were all that remained. The only evidence that part of my life had actually happened.

Would the world have been better off if I'd never existed? Is that what the point of this challenge was? To show me how many lives I'd ruined just by being here?

Leto would have agreed with Galen, Maddox and my father. That I was the cause of all their problems. She certainly thought I was the cause of all of her problems.

I kept walking, staying to the perimeter so that I didn't get lost within the alternate plane of existence. There was nothing. No buildings. No houses. No people. Just me.

And my thoughts.

I worked my way back to the spot where my father's house once stood and curled up on a patch of grass where my room would have been. I placed my hand on my belly, hoping to feel that first flicker of life that I'd felt back in Darius's cave.

But there was nothing.

It was as if my pregnancy never existed - because my relationship with Galen hadn't existed. Not in the way it had back in the real world.

A torrent of emotions blew up inside me - none of them good. All my failures and shortcomings. I relived every painful thing that had happened to me throughout the course of my life. From the smallest slight to major traumas. My nerves were beyond shot.

The psychological pain became so intense I felt it physically throughout my body like a crushing weight on my bones that took my breath away. My eyes burned from the excessive tears and my throat was raw from crying out until I'd lost my voice.

Even then the screaming didn't stop.

Muscle memory took over, going through the motions of producing a scream without any sound thanks to my damaged vocal chords. *At least they matched the rest of me.* I suffered in silence.

Which was a form of torture in and of itself.

"Talia?" A woman's voice pierced the solitude. Her words were almost musical, building from a single note to a symphony in the silence. "Is that you my darling?"

The voice was familiar, but from my past. At some level I recognized it, but it had been so long since I heard the sound I couldn't put a name or face to it - and that just made me sadder. The loss of that memory, the connection between this person and the sound of their voice hit me with such intensity it took my breath away.

"Talia." The woman reached for me, her smooth alabaster skin a stark contrast against the darkness encasing us. She stroked my hair and ran her hand down my back, rubbing in a large soothing circle. "It's mommy, sweetheart. Everything's all right. It's all going to be alright."

She shushed and cooed while she cradled me in her lap, comforting me the way she had when I was a little girl. I wanted to feel the joy of this reunion, of being with her again but all I felt was immeasurable loss for moments like these that were stolen from us when I was growing up, for the good and bad times we never experienced together.

And for it having been so long since I'd seen her, so long since I'd ever recalled the memories of her that I did have or thought of her beyond her connection to the Deofol pack and demon wolves, that I had forgotten the sound of her voice.

Or the warmth of her embrace.

I'd missed her so much. She'd missed out on so much and I wanted nothing more than to share those experiences with her. To tell her I understood what it was like to love someone so completely before you've ever seen their face or uttered their name.

But that future had been taken from me too.

"Talia, that future is still yours. You haven't lost anything, sweetheart." She took me by the arm, readjusting my position until my hand rested on my belly and then covered my hand with hers. "Block it all out. The negative voices in your head, the pain and sorrow. Block it all out and pull yourself out of the darkness. Don't think, just feel."

Easier said than done.

I'd been drowning in my emotions, pulled down like the La Brea tar pits, before my subconscious conjured the memory of my mother to save me from myself. I'd buried myself so deep in my feelings I wasn't sure that I could dig myself back out again.

Until I felt it.

A tiny flicker of life, of hope, within me. A physical manifestation of our love for each other - mine and Galen's - growing inside me. A new life that we created together.

"There now, you see. Just like I said," She stroked my hair, brushing an errant strand from my face and tucking it behind my ear. "Everything is going to be alright. Galen's still waiting for you on the other side of this. Right where you left him.

Though I think he might be a little worse for wear when you get back."

I doubted that very much. Galen was my rock. My alpha, my love. He gave me strength when I needed it, carried me when I wanted to quit and thought I couldn't go on. He could handle anything.

"Oh, my sweet girl." My mother's gentle laugh said I still had a lot to learn. "Wind and water will wear down the toughest stone over time. Men are fragile creatures."

Her words rang true, but Galen had to be the exception to the rule. I'd leaned on him far more than he'd leaned on me.

"You'll see." Her body vibrated with laughter and I knew she was smiling without having seen her face. "Trust me, you'll see."

"I've missed you so much, mom." I readjusted my position, rolling more to my side, and craned my neck so that I could look up at her.

She was beautiful. I wanted to add as I remembered but that would have been a lie. My father never talked about my mom. Her pictures had been taken down off the walls and mantle above the fireplace to be stored away. Our house had been scrubbed and sterilized of her image and over time that memory, the finer details of what she looked and sounded like began to fade away.

Her words hit home. Fragile creatures indeed.

"I missed you too, sweetheart, and as much as I would love to keep you with me, to catch up on all the precious time we lost, you can't stay here. You need to go back. Not just for him, or you, but for the life you created together. Your child will-"

"No more prophecies." I covered her mouth with my hand. "I've had my fill of destiny and fate."

"True enough," Her smile was infectious and so much like my own.

People always said I reminded them of her, but I never realized just how much I resembled her.

Or how much harder that must have been for my father. He'd tried so hard to get rid of the painful reminders but he couldn't get rid of me.

"It's time to go home, Talia. Galen's waiting for you and so is your future." She pulled me up, out of the darkness and back into the light.

Where my mate was waiting for me on the other side.

As much as I wanted to stay there with her, to reclaim the time and memories that had been stolen from us, I knew that if I stayed in the past, I'd be giving up my future.

"I'm going to miss you all over again." I wrapped my arms around her and pulled her into a hug.

"Not as much as I'll miss you." She hugged me back, and squeezed me tight, before easing back and taking me by the shoulder, holding me at arms length . "But you never really forgot me, did you? I've been with you your whole life."

She leaned in again and rested her forehead against mine. "Right here, all this time."

The darkness I'd entombed myself with began to fade with my mother's physical presence. The more light that poured into my heart and soul, the more translucent she became until she disappeared from my sight altogether. She was gone from the alternate reality, this dream that I'd created for myself.

But she wasn't gone this time. Not really. I'd rediscovered

her, the sound of her voice and details of her face, in the recesses of my mind. And she was there when I needed her. All I had to do was close my eyes.

My mother was right. It was time to pull myself out of the emotional muck that I'd dredged up and get back to my mate, to my life, to our future.

I'd faced down my own demons. It was time I did the same with Leto's.

# CHAPTER 11

# GALEN

Talia's voice had long since left her and the screams that pierced my heart as much as my ears had stopped. I'd wished for it, prayed to whatever gods were listening that her screaming would come to an end.

The silence was worse.

At least when she screamed, as tormented as she was, I knew that she was still there with me. A rational part that existed outside of the nightmare she was trapped in.

I knew my pain, the suffering I experienced on the sidelines, was nothing compared to whatever was happening inside Talia's own mind. More than once I considered throwing in the towel on her behalf. To save her from herself.

The only thing that stopped me was knowing that Talia would never forgive me.

Talia seized, followed by a series of small muscle tremors that worked their way across her body, and then she went rigid, board stiff with her limbs pinned at her sides.

I rushed over and cradled her frozen body in my arms as best I could. The rise and fall of her chest had slowed to a crawl, making it difficult to tell if she'd stopped breathing. I dipped my head, and leaned in, with my face close to hers and waited for the inhale and exhale of breath. My heart beat out of my chest, increasing in pace until I thought it might burst from my chest. Watching her suffer that way had been the most difficult thing I'd ever had to do.

There wasn't a clock in the temple, but I didn't need one to know how long it had been since Talia drank the tea and disappeared into herself. I'd counted down the minutes and hours until she woke up.

Three hours, fourteen minutes and twenty-seven seconds passed from the time Talia closed her eyes until I saw the first twitch and flutter of her eyelids - and my heart started beating again.

"Talia, can you hear me?" I brushed the back of my hand over her cheeks, caressing her skin. "Take a deep breath, baby. You're okay. Everything's going to be okay. I'm right here."

"Galen?" She blinked those wide, sapphire blue eyes at me, confusion swirling behind the glisten of formed tears.

It was the uncertainty that broke me all over again. As if she'd faced her own demons and fought her way out but was still uncertain if I would still be waiting for her when she came back.

She slid one arm around my waist and the other around the back of my neck and pulled me down until the tips of our noses touched.

"You're here." Her lips brushed mine when she spoke, the barest hint of a kiss. "I saw my mom."

"Yeah?" I kissed her lips, her brow, her cheek, leaving promises of things to come once she'd rested and regained her strength. "You'll have to tell me all about it."

I opened the bond and sent a push of energy her way. Enough to jump start her own healing process without overloading her system. She took that boost of energy and then some, reaching through the bond to spindle more energy for what she had planned next.

Talia communicated through our connection and gave me a heads up about her plans. She intended to claim her winnings right away, not wanting to give Leto a chance to welch on their deal.

But to do that she needed to replenish her strength before making her demands of the demon wolf goddess.

"Take what you need." I reached out through the pack bonds, tapped into the well of energy stored within our collective and opened the floodgates.

Talia no longer looked washed out or drained of color. Her skin was flushed and her natural glow restored. Her eyes brightened and spirits perked. The energy boost was just what she needed. If I hadn't witnessed it myself, I never would have believed she'd run a gauntlet of physical and mental trials back to back the way she had.

"I met the challenges you set before me and completed all three of your trials, Leto." Talia pushed to her feet, brushed herself off and moved to the center of the room. "We made a deal and I've kept up my end. Are you going to keep yours?"

She didn't bow, kneel or curtsey before the demon wolf goddess; choosing to stand at her full height with her head held high as if she was Leto's equal.

In my eyes she was.

Talia was a warrior, a goddess, my mate and the mother of my child. No woman, demon wolf goddess or otherwise could hold a candle to her.

"Are you insinuating that I would not uphold the terms of our agreement?" Leto met our skeptical gazes with a knowing smile. "Your suspicion has been hard earned, but I assure you my word is bond. You bested my warrior, returned from conquest with Artemis's arrowhead, defeated your inner demons and were victorious in the third trial. Your heart is true and so are your words."

"Thank you goddess." Talia dipped her head, tucking her chin against her chest and bowed at her waist. "Galen and I are grateful for your help getting rid of the demons, but I would appreciate getting rid of these marks first."

Talia made a graceful transition from bowing to standing at her full height. She pointed to the marks made by Lupercus, the demon wolf god, on her skin.

"I know you are eager to remove my husband's claim on you, and nothing would give me greater pleasure than removing Lupercus's mark from your body, but it requires a moon ritual."

Leto rose from her throne and glided down the dais stairs, crossing the room to a pedestal in the upper left corner. She ran the tip of her index finger across her tongue and flipped through the pages of the old leather bound tome.

"Here it is. The ceremony is simple enough and there will be plenty of moon light as the spell requires. My priestesses will gather the necessary supplies and make the preparations. " She ran her hand down the center of the book, applying pressure to encourage the book to remain open. "As for the demons, eradicating them will not be as simple."

"You mean, they don't listen to you?" I asked, baffled by the revelation. I'd assumed they were under her control, and unable to refuse her. "But, you sent them. So wouldn't you just call them back or something?"

I'd hoped we hadn't traveled all the way to Alaska, survived the demon wolf pack, Darius's betrayals, not to mention the challenges Talia had to face on her own, for nothing. We'd put all our eggs into one basket. It was too late to change course and try something else.

If Leto couldn't help us, the world as we knew it was over.

"I am not the only supreme being that they listen to. I could stop them and you could return to your home, only to find that the demons had been given a new directive and done the same." She ran her finger over the ancient text, mouthing the words as she read the ceremonial words to herself. "Lupercus could and would unravel my spells, making all of this for naught."

Leto unfastened the silk sash draped over her shoulder and offered it to Talia, who then wrapped it around herself and tucked it in at the end like a beach towel.

"I definitely didn't go through all of this just to have the demon wolf god come in and claim victory at the end. Whatever we do, it needs to be Lupercus proof." Talia checked the sash where she'd tucked it in, making sure it wouldn't unravel.

"What do we need to do? I'll do whatever it takes." I put emphasis on the word I.

Talia had done more than her share of the heavy lifting. She didn't need to do any more. I was more than willing to step in and step up.

"I appreciate, as I'm sure your mate does as well, your willingness to make an offering on her behalf, but once again, alpha, the sacrifice isn't yours to make."

Leto rested a firm hand on my shoulder. She seemed to be aiming for a comforting gesture but landed hard on menacing instead.

"Revoking demons requires demon blood. Demon wolf blood specifically." The demon wolf goddess pulled a blade from the folds of her skirt, grabbed Talia's hand and ran the edge across her palm before either of us knew what happened. "Once upon a time, demon wolves used to herd the demon hordes for us, driving them back behind the barriers between worlds."

"Why did they stop?" Talia seemed interested in what the goddess had to say about the history of the demon wolf clans.

Not that I blamed her, neither of us had heard this particular story before.

"Times change. So do beliefs." The demon wolf goddess produced a small silver chalice to collect Talia's blood and a piece of gauze to bind the wound once she finished. "This should do it."

The bowl was near to overflowing by the time Leto wrapped the gauze around Talia's hand. I hoped Leto had collected enough because there was no way Talia could donate any more. She'd gone white as a sheet and swayed side to side on her feet.

"Can you shift?" I rested a hand on each of her shoulders and steadied her. When Talia's knees wobbled, I scooped her up in my arms and cradled her against my chest. "Maybe you should rest for a few minutes and then shift."

"We're trying to limit my shifts, remember? Until we get home and talk to the midwife." Talia had been such a badass, fighting her way out of the Deofol pack, Darius and Leto's challenges, that I almost forgot what a fragile state she was in.

We'd agreed that until we'd met with the Long Claw midwife, and determined how the transformations would affect the baby's development that Talia would only shift when necessary. Minor blood loss and exhaustion wasn't anything that couldn't be cured with a good meal, a lot of water and a long nap. She could do all of those things in her human form.

"I'll send one of my priestesses to check on you. Alita will escort you to my chambers. You can rest there until the preparations for tonight's ritual are complete." Leto motioned for Alita to come forward, repeating her instructions for the captain of her guard.

As you command, my goddess." Alita rested her hand on the pommel of her sword and guided the sheathed blade behind her as she dropped into a low bow, where she remained until Leto dismissed her. "Follow me."

The leader of the shieldmaidens escorted us across the throne room to the rear exit at the back of the temple. There was a matching set of stairs to the one at the main temple entrance, but these didn't lead to the market or village below, but to a small villa nestled between an olive grove and a lemon orchard with views overlooking the cliffs and a vast ocean.

"You fought well today, princess." Alita ushered us inside the goddess's villa and into a spacious living room. "One of the acolytes will be here shortly with fresh food, water and a change of clothes for the both of you. Please, enjoy the goddess's hospitality."

It felt like there was an unspoken *"while it lasts"* hanging in the air between us. Still, Talia needed rest and recuperation and I was grateful for the use of the goddess's villa while we waited for the temple priestesses to finish their preparations.

"Alita." Talia called after the leader of the shieldmaidens, stopping her before she left the villa and returned to her guard duties at the temple. "You are a true warrior. I could learn a lot from you and your shieldmaidens."

"Perhaps one day we will have the honor of teaching you." The hard lines of Alita's face softened. It was as close to a smile as I'd seen from the captain of the guard. She nodded her good-byes to both of us and took her leave.

The villa was an open floor plan with each room spilling into the other. Oversized pillows and cushions encased with silk in rich, warm reds and burnt oranges were scattered about the villa in place of chairs or couches. It felt lush and decadent, yet completely casual.

The living room opened up to an outdoor patio with a fire pit and an infinity pool that had a built-in jacuzzi.

"What do you think? Inside or out?" I would have chosen the patio but I left it up to Talia.

So many choices had been taken away from her that even something as simple as where we sat probably felt like a big decision. I wanted her to have some semblance of control over her life, even if it was just choosing between a living room and a patio.

Especially while so much of our lives was still outside of our control.

"I know it's warmer here than Alaska, so it's probably not necessary, but I would love to be outside and just curl up by the fire. Maybe watch the sunset." Talia cupped my face in her hands and claimed my mouth with a kiss.

I returned the kiss, but didn't deepen it, waiting for Talia to make the next move. We either kicked up the heat or we didn't. It was up to her. I was happy to have her in my arms whether I was comforting her, or making love to her.

Either way, we were together and that was all that mattered to me.

"I should be okay to walk on my own." Talia kissed my forehead, my cheek, and nipped at my lips one more time before I set her down.

She took her time getting out to the patio, but she kept her footing while I hovered behind her ready to catch her if she fell. I busied myself arranging logs in the firepit while Talia arranged the cushions and stacked a few pillows. Before long we were nestled up by a cozy fire with a platter of sliced breads, dried meats, fruits, nuts and cheeses, and a carafe of cool mineral water.

It was a complete three-sixty from where we'd been when we first arrived and even more so from the reception we'd received from the Deofol pack.

"Say what you want about her, and I know there's a lot to say," Talia said with a heart filled laugh. "But the goddess has good taste."

"Good taste in cheese, maybe." I teased. "But her taste in husbands..."

It was a good thing Talia's seat was already on the floor or she would have fallen off the cushion when she doubled over with laughter. Her good mood and boisterous laughs were contagious. We joked around, cracking each other up with dad jokes and cheesy punch lines until our sides hurt and we had tears in our eyes.

The stitch in my side was a welcomed pain - especially compared to the injuries we'd sustained over the previous weeks. It was good to see her lit up with a genuine smile, to hear her laughter fill the quiet of the early evening.

I caught a glimpse of our future together, filled with so much joy. You couldn't have one without the other. We knew that better than most. But there would always be laughter, even through the tears.

And love. So much love.

We talked for hours about everything. All the conversations we hadn't had time to have while we ran from one catastrophe or crisis to the next. No topic was off limits. We memorized each other's favorite foods, colors, and songs.

And favorite baby names.

She sat by the fire, basking in its light and warmth, making lists of names - one for a girl and one for a boy - while I fell in love with her all over again.

The sun was well below the horizon, making way for the moon and stars. Leto and her priestesses should have had everything prepared for the ritual to remove Lupercus's marks from Talia. She was so close to being free of his claim on her.

The nightmare was almost over.

Almost.

# CHAPTER 12

# TALIA

I could have stayed on the patio by the fire talking with Galen forever. If not for the ceremony to remove the demon wolf god's marks on my body and claim on my soul, I might have. It felt like an eternity since my heart felt that light and was as close to heaven as I'd ever been.

And I had a lifetime of nights like that ahead of me.

All the more reason to return to the temple and perform Leto's ritual to free my body and soul from Lupercus.

The demon wolf goddess was almost ready. She sent an acolyte down to the villa with specific instructions on how to prepare for the ritual before arriving at the temple and ceremonial midnight blue robes made of the finest silk - one for each of us.

The acolyte set the robes aside and retrieved a hand full of incense cones from a leather pouch fastened to the rope belt around her waist. She asked us to remove our clothes while she set the incense in a glass dish, lit them on fire, blowing them out when the tips turned cherry red.

The goddess's devotee held her face close to the dish, blowing on the incense until a strong plume of smoke wafted up from the cones. She walked around each of us in a counter-clockwise circle and then retraced her steps, raising and lowering the incense as she went until our bodies were covered in the cloying scent of cloves and orange blossoms.

Galen and I covered ourselves with the robes and followed the acolyte up to the temple where the goddess and her priestesses waited for us. Her throne had been removed and a long table took its place.

Wrought iron standing candelabras that held four white taper candles were placed around the room, casting a soft, soothing glow against the cold marble used to construct her temple.

"Talia Ciletti, child of the Deofol wolves, Princess of the Bone clan, have you come to seek the help of Leto, Goddess of the Demon Wolves of your own accord?" A priestess dressed in an emerald green robe opened her arms in a sweeping gesture, then motioned for me to come forward and join the goddess at the table.

A satin runner in a shade of green similar to the priestesses robes was laid out over the tabletop and adorned with wolf idols carved from wood and stone. More pillar candles, clustered in groups of three, were placed on the middle and ends of the table.

The priestess nudged me forward and gave two quick nods, encouraging me to answer the question she posed about my intentions for being in the temple and performing the ceremony.

"I do." Dressed in a blue robe, standing beside an elderly woman with skin drawn tight over fragile bones and long silver braids plated down her back wasn't how I envisioned myself saying those words.

"The ritual requires a sacrifice." The goddess came to my side and handed me an athame adorned with a large opal in the pommel. "A small prick, just a few drops of blood will suffice."

"Oh, good." I took the knife, turning it in my hands, as I approached the altar. "You had me worried there for a second."

"You've given enough blood for one night, but rituals are as much about precision as intent. There are no shortcuts for you to reach your desired results. You have to start at the beginning before you can reach the end." The demon wolf goddess stepped behind a podium that held the ancient texts that broke down the steps we needed to take to perform the ritual.

She waited for me to prick my finger on the athame and sprinkle a few drops of my blood over the altar before she read the rites from the leather bound tome. The candles flickered once, twice, before the flames grew three times their normal size.

"The offering has been accepted." Leto turned the page in her book and began reading from the text.

She spoke her lines and the acolytes repeated them. Each time they spoke the words with more intensity, more emphasis and increased speed until it became a chant at a fevered pitch. The women rocked back and forth, saying the words over and over.

Again the candle flames shot up toward the ceiling.

The skin on my arm forearm where the first mark had been placed itched and then burned. The ink of the symbol turned from black to an angry red. Smoke wafted off my skin and the area around the mark began to bubble up with blisters that split and cracked.

Instinct drove my hand to the blistering wound to cover it and prevent any more damage, but the acolytes grabbed my wrists and held my arms out in front of me. Galen rushed to my side, unsure of how to help, but his presence was enough to remind me why I was doing this and what was at stake if I didn't go through with it.

"It's working." More than half the mark had already disappeared from my forearm. "Galen, it's working. She's doing it."

We'd tried everything to remove the mark. Even the high priestess of our local coven had failed where Leto succeeded. I was finally going to be free of the demon wolf god's marks.

But Lupercus would not let me go so easily.

White wolves, with blazing red eyes, charged into the temple and attacked the acolytes. Alita and the shieldmaidens rushed in with their swords drawn and shields raised but they were too late to save their goddess's followers.

Leto was forced to stop the ritual and defend her temple from an attack by the Deofol pack. Lupercus was close. I felt his increasing presence through the second mark which had yet to fade.

"Galen, he's here." I managed to warn my true mate seconds before the demon wolf god exploded onto the scene and overturned the altar.

"I see that." Galen moved in front of me, using his body to shield me from Lupercus's wrath.

Which, for the moment, was directed at his wife.

"Leto, you dare to interfere with my plans?" Lupercus's full form materialized in the throne room. "Your jealousy has grown tiresome over the years. I've grown bored with you, pet. Though raising a demon horde was a new twist on an old game. I admit, it caught me by surprise at first. I thought one of my creatures had stirred an uprising, but they would dare."

It was the first time I'd laid eyes on him.

The demon wolf god was handsome, with raven black hair, a strong jaw, full lips, and a chiseled physique. I supposed a woman could do worse than Lupercus – until he opened his mouth and every arrogant thought in his head came pouring out. Still, it was easy to understand how Leto had fallen for and become so jealous of her husband.

But my heart didn't belong to him. It belonged to Galen.

Members of the Deofol pack, Lupercus's most devoted followers, had slaughtered the acolytes and defiled Leto's temple. She let out a ferocious growl that would have rivalled any wolf in our pack, her eyes taking on a yellowish glow that I'd seen in the eyes of every pack member I'd ever known. Leto's body never shifted but she in every other way, she looked and sounded every bit a wild wolf.

Leto proved why she had been given the title of the wolf goddess.

She lashed out at the first demon wolf who crossed her path, slicing through its thick coat, into muscle and through bone with ease. She tossed the carcass aside and moved on to the next. Leto was covered in blood and gore, but it didn't seem to bother her. She was a warrior as well as a goddess.

Two more wolves split off from the Deofol pack and lunged in my direction. Galen shifted. I felt him pull on our bond and that of the pack which had been growing stronger ever since I completed the third challenge.

His wolf bursting out from his skin in under a minute. He charged after the two wolves, attacking them before they could reach me.

But that wasn't why the demon wolf god unleashed them in the temple.

The whole thing was one big diversion. Lupercus sent his wolves to distract Galen and his wife and set his sights on me.

"You belong to me, princess." The demon wolf god grabbed my arm, just below the mark his wife began to successfully remove before he'd interrupted the ritual. "You can try to remove the marks all you want, princess, but the fact remains. You are mine. Her attempts to stop me have failed before and she would have failed with you."

"No." I dug my claws into the top of his hand and raked them through skin and muscle. "I won't go with you. I don't belong to you and I'm not your mate."

I fought against his hold, shifting my weight to one side for leverage as I tried to yank myself free.

"You dare to defy me? No one refuses me." Lupercus growled. The demon wolf god reared back, shocked that I refused his unsolicited offer to make me his mate. "I am the demon wolf god, no one refuses me. No one."

"Well, someone had to be first. It might as well be me. I am refusing you because I am not in love with you." I did a quick scan of the room, searching for Galen to make sure that he was okay. It took a moment to find him in the fray. My heart resumed its rhythm once I spotted him. "I tried to tell Darius before he pulled me through that portal, but he didn't listen and look what happened to him.

Galen fought side by side with Leto, who was mid strike, slaying through one of the wolves that killed the priestesses who were assisting in the ceremony. They had their hands full thinning the pack that had destroyed the temple and I wouldn't risk their safety by distracting them with a cry for help.

The ritual had removed enough of the mark that I could fight against the demon wolf god while maintaining my free will. Something that his other "*wives*" had been unable to do.

Which was more confirmation that despite their difficulty, I'd made the right choice when I accepted Leto's challenges and bargained for her help. There would have been no consort agreement, no reprieve from the demon wolf god's obsessive affection.

"Are you seriously threatening me?" Lupercus asked, through his laughter. "I am a god. Mortal whims aren't enough to stop me. And if you meant to shock me with news of Darius's demise, you're too late. I have already learned of his failures."

Lupercus wasn't fazed at all by the loss of one of his demon wolves. They were replaceable to him. When one died another stepped up to the plate to replace them. Darius had a higher position with the demon wolf pack, but he was no different than the rest – dispensable.

The demon wolf god grabbed my hair and pulled me toward him. His arm wrapped around my midsection, pinning me in place against the hard planes of his body. I heard the sharp intake of breath when he felt the faint flutter of life within me.

"I should be upset over this infidelity, princess. With any of my other mates I would have been, but with you I find myself excited to learn of your fertility. I may even let you keep the pup when its born if you behave." He splayed his fingers across my stomach. "You will bear me an heir. A demigod among men."

Leto must have overheard her husband's plans to use me as a broodmare, to produce a demigod heir to his throne, because she stopped mid fight, turned her attention from the demon wolf snapping its jaws at her feet and focused on her husband. She stomped on the wolf, walking over it like her husband had over the shards of the heart and mind he'd broken with his indifference and infidelity.

"Lupercus." The demon wolf goddess called to her husband. "This has gone far enough. Our marital problems and meddling have caused enough problems for the mortal world."

The demon wolves destroyed her temple. Cracks in the marble floor and walls undermined the integrity of the structure. They'd reduced her grand structure to just another mythological ruin scattered about in Greece or Rome.

"Call off your dogs, husband." Leto raised her arm to her side, caught another of the demon wolves mid air as it lunged for her and snapped its neck. She tossed the carcass on the floor like a wad of paper.

But the demon wolf god refused her and opened a portal instead. He was about to drag me through when Galen stopped him.

"I challenge you, Lupercus. A match to first blood." Galen

threw his challenge down at the demon wolf god's feet and waited for an answer.

Lupercus didn't respond. He called back his wolves with the snap of his fingers and commanded them to heel in front of me, forming a wall of fur and muscle to block me off from Galen and even Leto - who had somehow become our ally in our fight against her husband.

It seemed her blame had finally been placed where it belonged – with her husband.

My heart stopped. Galen was an incredible fighter. He was also a leader and if he fell so did the rest of the Long Claw pack back home. Galen's pack had been holding the demon hordes. Challenging Lupercus was a huge risk, especially when we were so close to getting what we needed, but I trusted my mate to do what he thought was best.

Even if what he thought was best, was fighting with a god.

# CHAPTER 13

# GALEN

First blood. There was only one rule to the challenge and it was in the name. Whichever opponent drew first blood won. The stakes were higher than just my pack which would have been bad enough, But Talia and our baby were on the line.

Not to mention the cities and towns surrounding the Long Claw pack. They suffered right along with us.

"You're offering me the opportunity to rid myself of the one major obstacle standing in the way of my union with the Bone Clan Princess?" Lupercus's laughter seemed genuine.

"I am."

My challenge amused the demon wolf god. I supposed that if I were in his position I would feel the same way.

I was close to immortal when compared to a regular human, but compared to Lupercus? I might as well have been a mortal. My speed and agility, increased strength and rapid regeneration were considered scientific marvels back home, but against a god? They weren't even considered an advantage.

I wasn't sure which was more dangerous. A man with nothing to lose and everything to gain. Or a man with everything to lose.

Talia and I were going to start a family - with a baby already on the way. It seemed like overnight our future became our present. I had everything I ever wanted, more actually, with Talia as my mate. I couldn't afford to lose her, our child or our life together. I wasn't as strong as her and I knew I wouldn't survive it.

No, the only way to secure our future, make it ironclad was to take down Lupercus.

Whether I won or lost the challenge against the demon wolf god, would come down to brains and not brawn. It had to be about strategy. That was the only way that I was going to defeat him.

"Very well. I accept. Take a moment to mentally prepare yourself. I've heard defeat is difficult to process." Lupercus released Talia from his hold, but not before he reminded her of where she was going or who she was going home with at the end of the challenge. "Take a moment to say your goodbyes. We'll be leaving this place immediately following my victory."

The demon wolf god's arrogance would be his downfall.

A few of Lupercus's minions from the Deofol pack lumbered into what was left of Leto's throne room and cleared away the bodies and the debris. When the marble floor had been cleaned to their god's satisfaction, they slipped back into the shadows.

Talia sprinted across the room and rushed into my open arms.

"Galen, are you sure you want to do this?" She buried her face in the crook of my neck to hide her tears, but her sniffles gave her away. "Leto agreed to help us and after what the Deofol pack did to her temple, she's definitely on our side."

"Leto and Lupercus are only ever on their own side. She put you through the ringer before she would even raise a finger to help you knowing damn well you didn't do anything to provoke this." I held her close, tightening my hold until all of her curves were molded to my body. "It's been you and me from the start of this and that's how it's going to end."

"Make him bleed, Galen." Talia cupped my face in her hands and drew me in for a kiss. "Let's finish this."

"Princess Talia, if you would join your brethren from the Bone Clan on the opposite side of the room, we will be able to leave that much sooner." Lupercus stalked her movements with his gaze like a predator on the prowl for its next meal.

Leto's ritual may have partially removed his mark, making it unrecognizable to anyone outside of the Deofol pack and their gods, but the demon wolf god had other ways of claiming my mate for his own.

But he needed to get through me first, and I wasn't going to make it easy for him.

Lupercus and I stood at opposite ends of the room, treating the center space as our unofficial fighting ring. Bjorn was in the demon wolf god's corner and Leto was in mine.

Having a goddess in my corner felt like an advantage over an alpha, but there was only so much Leto could do to help me. I was less interested in her healing abilities since the challenge I'd selected was unlike any other.

It was one round, one good hit to draw first blood.

Had I challenged Lupercus to a traditional multi round fight as most wolves do when making a play to overthrow their alpha, her skills with bandages and salves would have come in handy. But what interested me more for this particular challenge was her knowledge of her husband.

And the goddess did not disappoint.

Her insight on the way he moved, his fighting style and techniques, was invaluable. If Lupercus landed a hit and drew first blood, then it was all on me, because Leto had done everything she could to help me.

The demon wolf goddess had indeed had a change of heart.

"Thank you, Leto. Talia and I appreciate your help. Truly." I tucked my chin against my chest and bent at the waist in a brief bow.

"If I thought otherwise, you wouldn't be on the receiving end of it." Leto draped her arm around my shoulders in a sideways embrace. "I should have offered it sooner and without condition, alpha. For that I am sorry."

I expressed my gratitude once more before joining her husband out in the middle of the marble floor.

"I believe we can skip the formalities." Lupercus dropped into a fighting stance, ready to launch an offensive attack.

"Whenever you're ready." I widened my stance and raised my arms, elbows tucked in towards my sides, in a defensive stance.

Leto suggested letting him make the first move. It played to his ego and right into my hands when he left himself open to an attack. I took her advice and waited for the demon wolf god to come to me.

His movements were slower than I would have expected,

more pronounced and easy to predict. As powerful as he was, I could only assume that he'd grown accustomed to having demons and demon wolves do his dirty work.

It must have been a long time since Lupercus had been in hand to hand combat. He needed time to shake off the ring rust, but time wasn't something he had enough of. He had one round in the ring. One chance to draw blood.

The same as me.

Watching him lumber through his punches, I knew I'd made the right choice with a first blood challenge.

I dipped, dodged, and used footwork to own the ring and avoid his blows. There weren't any breaks, no time to rest or catch your breath. The second part of my strategy had been to wear him down.

Lupercus came at me again, and again I dodged the blow. But this time I tapped a skill at every alpha's disposal and partially shifted my hand. With my claws extended, I threw a counterpunch, digging in with my nails on the end of the swing.

Bright red welts formed. The demon wolf god's blood spilled over the deep scratches and streaked down his cheek.

"First blood." I retracted my claws and backed up toward the edge of the makeshift ring.

The injury to his face had already begun to heal. The injury to his pride on the other hand would take much longer. I got the impression the demon wolf god was used to getting his way. Losing wasn't something he was accustomed to.

Or knew how to do it gracefully.

One of the priestesses in service of the goddess shouted

something, but I couldn't make out what she said. A few of the other devotees in the room shouted as well and that time I heard the warning for what it was. I turned in time to see the glint of light on hardened steel as Lupercus pulled his arm back, readied to drive the blade into my back.

Leto jumped in, shoved me out of the way and grabbed her husband's wrist. The muscles in her forearm twitched as she held her husband back, staving off an attack after the challenge had ended and from the blade from being buried in my shoulder blade.

Lupercus landed a back hand across his wife's cheek. I scrambled out of the way, grabbed Talia by the hand and led her to the opposite side of the temple from the demon wolf god and goddess, and out of the crossfire zone.

Leto unleashed a lifetime of fury on her husband. Landing blow after blow until he collapsed on his knees before huddling on the floor at her feet.

"Free her from the last mark." Leto pressed her heel against Lupercus's throat, increasing weight and pressure until her husband complied with her command and released Talia from his mark and any false claims he'd placed on her.

Talia turned her arm, twisting in every direction she could to look at it from every angle possible. The demon wolf god's mark was gone without a trace. There were no blisters or burns, no welts or scar tissue. The skin on her forearm was as smooth and perfect as the rest of her.

The second mark disappeared and left the skin unmarred the same way as the first.

She was free of him at last. Tears glistened in her sapphire blue eyes, spilling over her lush lashes to track down her cheeks. Her smile had been captivating before, but in that moment, I realized I'd never experienced it in its full effect. A cloud had hung over her even on our happier days, but with the demon wolf god's marks gone, those bonds broken, I saw what pure joy looked like on my mate's face.

I swore to devote myself to making sure Talia experienced that same joy every day for the rest of our lives.

In place of the demon god's mark, a new pattern appeared on her forearm. A crescent moon with a single star. The mark appeared to form from liquid silver and stardust, in smooth perfect lines that shimmered like the moon's reflection on still water.

"Galen, look." Talia gasped as she watched the lines close and complete the shape. "Is this-"

"Our fated mate mark." A carbon copied design, just smaller in size appeared on the skin between my forefinger and thumb.

I knew how relieved Talia was to see our mark, a physical manifestation of the love we shared and the life we created, but I didn't need it to tell me how I felt about her. She was, is, always would be the love of my life. Talia hung the moon as far as I was concerned and our fated mark no matter how unnecessary I felt it was, was still a perfect fit.

It turned out that Maddox never was Talia's fated mate and while I'll never understand why they perpetuated that lie or why the Northwood alpha wanted his heir to marry a wolf he hated and seemed unworthy, the truth was, Maddox was the wolf lacking not Talia. She was never a rejected mate.

Lupercus took advantage of Talia's vulnerable state after her heartbreak and put his plan in motion to take her for his new bride by claiming she was his mate. The spell he used to have his marks appear on her body, masked the true fated mate mark.

Mine and Talia's.

We were meant to be. It was in the stars and on our skin for anyone who needed more proof. Talia had left her mark on my heart and while I couldn't show that one off to my packmates or anyone who made eyes at my mate, that was the mark I was truly proud of.

Leto congratulated us on our mating bond and receiving the mark. But she stopped there and never made it as far as apologizing or accepting her responsibility for the role she played in the demon hordes destroying our home town and towns like it all over the country. Still, she created the potions that will help us banish the demons and seal any portals that remained open.

Lupercus called his demon minions to his side and opened a portal. The center of the gateway was an inky black, thick liquid with slow rolling ripples that moved across its surface. The demon wolf god pressed the tip of his finger to the center of the liquid. The waves stilled and the liquid thinned from a opaque tar to a translucent gray water, and revealed Lupercus's home on the other side of the portal. The demon wolf god left his wife's temple defeated, humiliated and without a new mate to add to his collection.

It was the ending he deserved.

Talia and I were nowhere near the end of our journey. There

was a lot of work to be done back home ridding the town of the demon hordes. Something they couldn't do without us and the solution that Leto made from Talia's blood.

It was high time we headed home - to kick some demon ass.

# CHAPTER 14
## TALIA

Home sweet home. I was glad to be back on Long Claw land - and so were my toes which still felt like they were frozen. I wasn't sure if I would ever thaw out.

Alaska put us through the ringer, but it had been a necessary trip for the future of our relationship and for the pack. But now that we were back, there was more work to be done.

Galen met with his betas to ensure that Darius's infiltration of the pack on behalf of the demon wolf god, Lupercus, didn't extend beyond an interest in me. He'd seen our pack's strengths and weaknesses. If he'd wanted to expand his demon wolves from the frozen terrain in northernmost Alaska, our pack would have been a good place to start.

Especially with my heritage, blood ties and the mating bond with the alpha of the Long Claw pack.

"Man, are we glad you're back." Theo clapped a hand on

Galen's shoulder before pulling him to in a brief hug. "We lost track of you after Anchorage. A storm moved in and-"

"And stayed in." Marcus extended his hand for Galen, who'd disentangled himself from Theo. They clasped each other's forearms in a firm grip, shook and a quick hug. "We tried everything to hire a pilot, but no one would take off in that weather. Said we were nuts for even thinking about it."

"I thought Marcus was going to shift right then and there." David gave a hearty laugh and clapped Marcus on the back before tugging Galen into a side hug.

"I'm surprised he didn't." Galen joined in teasing one of his betas and the four of them fell into their regular rhythm.

The relief in the room was palpable – and through the pack bonds. Galen and I had been to hell and back, but his men had their share of trouble too. Not being able to help their alpha being chief among them.

"For a woman who's been kidnapped and almost married off to a demon wolf god, you are positively glowing, Talia." Theo's observant gaze seemed to penetrate right through me. "My sister had that same look when she was...No. No way. Are you?"

He turned to Galen and grabbed his hand.

"Congratulations." He shook Galen's hand with vigor and glanced back at me with an ear-to-ear grin like he was the expectant father and not his alpha. "Uncle Theo. Has a nice ring to it. So does godfather."

He said the last in a terrible, husky Italian accent and horrible impersonation from the iconic movie.

"Wait, what?" David and Marcus parroted each other. "You're going to have a baby?"

Galen nodded, beaming as he flashed our mating mark permanently inked on his skin through our mated bond.

The three of them argued for a few minutes about who would be the baby's favorited uncle before Galen tabled the friendly debate after deeming it unwinnable.

"You'll just have to wait until after the baby is old enough to decide for him-or-her-self." He was still smiling when he brought the reunion to its real purpose.

Darius.

Much to my relief - and Galen's - Lupercus hadn't set his sights on the pack. At least not yet. After the humiliating loss he'd suffered at the hands of my mate, only time would tell if he decided to exact some kind of revenge for some imagined slight.

Galen put in a call to the Alliance, informing them of some of the details of our Alaskan adventure. He'd decided it was best to leave any of the details about my heritage or that I'd caught the interest of the demon wolf god and the ire of his wife. He seemed concerned about their politics and need for a place to lay the blame.

I reminded him that the blame lay squarely at Lupercus's feet – and Bjorn's. Galen reminded me that a god wasn't punishable under the packs' laws, but I was. If the alliance were looking for a scapegoat, he had no intentions of putting me in their cross hairs.

Especially when it was my blood that was used in the potion Leto conjured to destroy the demons she'd raised.

It might raise questions. Questions they may not believe the answers to. Did the potion work both ways? If my blood could send them back, could it raise them to? The answer was no. But after the attacks the alliance was unlikely to take any chances.

In the end, I couldn't argue with his logic and agreed some-things were better left unsaid when it came to the political figureheads who served on the alliance councils.

Galen gave them as much information as he could, leaving out any mention of me – or the potion.

At least until after we'd tested it and found a way to repli-cate it without my blood.

We spared a few minutes and stopped by the cemetery to pay our respects to Max. I knew how much it pained Galen to not be able to share the news of our mating bond and baby on the way with his father. Neither of my parents were alive to share in our joy or the experience of having a grandchild. Fortu-nately for our baby, life in a pack meant plenty of adoptive grandparents, aunts, uncles, and cousins. He or she was sure to be spoiled with love no matter what.

Of course, we were still in the first trimester and had a long way to go. There was plenty of time for picking out godparents, baby showers or building a crib.

Before we baby proofed our lives, we needed to baby proof our town - and that meant cleaning up the demon mess Leto and Lupercus made.

We decided to test the ritual and solution Leto gave us before sharing the process with the national pack alliance or any of Galen's allies. Especially since the solution Leto made contained a large amount of my blood. That wasn't something I was willing to just give to anyone without making sure it worked and we kept control of it.

The one exception to that had been Marguerite. It seemed

counterintuitive to give a witch anything that contained my blood considering their vast knowledge of potions and spells. It wouldn't have been hard for them to trace the magic further back than my bloodline. But we trusted her and her coven to create a blind replication ensuring we had enough to place seals and sigils on buildings throughout town and on any portals that remained open.

Leto had given us a banishment spell to share with the coven and they had already made preparations for their own mass ritual to send any demons trapped on our side of the portal back to the realm of the demon wolf god and goddess where they belonged.

It took a few weeks of replacing the sigils, reworking any necessary wards, and Marguerite and her coven performing the ritual to cleanse Long Claw lands and the town of the demon scourge.

Dozens of townspeople had been possessed in our absence which slowed the process. They needed to be exorcised from their human hosts before the potion could be used to send them back to hell. Marguerite, Sarah, and the rest of the coven worked on a spell that separated the two and prevented the demon from re-entering once they'd been evicted from the human's soul.

The witches also replicated Leto's concoction, with a few added ingredients to mask my blood and reduce the amount needed to make a potion. Only a few drops were required compared to the pint the demon wolf goddess had used. It wasn't as strong, which meant a larger batch had to be brewed to expel all of the demons that had infiltrated our community.

There were more demons than when we'd set out for Alaska.

I would have been more than happy to contribute as much Marguerite needed for a stronger potion, but the high priestess and Galen didn't want to risk the baby – or the alliance discovering the secret ingredient.

The less the wolf council knew about my ties to the demon pack and their gods, the better.

Galen waited until the sun had set and they were under the cover of darkness before heading into town with the potion and a handful of wolves, Markus and David included. Theo had been ordered to stay behind and watch over the pack in case a demons tried to breach the wards for one last attack.

But I saw right through my mate.

The pack members were tired, and our numbers had thinned since the first demon sighting, but they were Long Claw and more than capable of defending themselves if we were attacked.

In truth, Theo stayed behind to keep an eye on me.

Galen ordered me to stay home and while I bristled at his tone and considered launching an objection to being sidelined, I decided against it. We'd been partners in everything since Galen first plucked me off the street and the whole nightmare between packs and demons began, but our pack members weren't the only ones who were tired.

Our alpha was too.

He'd put himself second to me and our pack, not sleeping or eating like he should, and I knew how deeply the losses of his father and every wolf under his protection affected him.

They'd taken a toll – so had losing me to the Deofol pack, Darius, and the demon wolf god.

Losing me and the baby wasn't a risk he was willing to take.

I wanted to help, ached to fight alongside him and do my part in banishing the demons – especially since I was the reason they'd been raised in the first place. But my presence would have been more of a distraction. One Galen couldn't afford. I didn't want his attention split between protecting himself and his wolves, or me and the baby. I knew who he'd choose if forced to decide and I couldn't live with that on my conscience.

I spared his pride and his nerves and stayed behind.

Under Marguerite's command, the coven armed themselves with another batch of the potion and followed Galen into town. Knowing he had back up gave me some peace of mind, but I wouldn't be able to relax until he was back home with me, safe and sound, where he belonged.

The solution Marguerite drafted from Leto's original recipe had done the trick. Our streets were clear and the people had returned to their lives. Businesses reopened and families moved back to their homes. We finally had peace.

Well, some peace.

The demons were gone which meant life had slowly returned to normal - and that included the Northwood pack's attempts to take control over ours. Maddox and his father never learned from their mistakes before. It seemed naive of me to expect them to just up and change their ways. But if anything could have done that it would have been a bunch of demons running loose.

When that failed, it was clear that the Northwood pack was

well and truly hopeless under their current leadership. If it could even be called leadership. Tyranny was closer to the truth.

Galen and I stayed up with the sunrise several nights discussing what, if any, our next move would be with the Northwood pack. They'd wasted no time attacking us once word got out that we'd returned home from Alaska as fated mates with a baby on the way.

It seemed Maddox and his father would not stop until they'd taken me out.

A pack war wasn't part of the plans that Galen and I made for our future, which left us with no other choice but to take over the Northwood pack and merge them with the Long Claw pack.

It was a win-win scenario, and we presented it as such to Galen's betas and the pack elders. This decision affected the entire pack, and it was important to us both that they had an opportunity to hear our thoughts on a pack merger and give them an opportunity to share theirs in return.

It wasn't often an alpha asked for advice from his pack-mates, much less heeded it, but Galen wasn't just another alpha. He cared about his pack and every wolf in it. All the more reason to bring the Northwoods into the fold.

At least the ones worth saving.

There were good people in my old pack. Trapped in between a rock and a hard place with the current leadership and nowhere else to go.

We were about to change that.

The Northwood pack crossed our property lines and

launched attack, after attack on our people. Spilling innocent blood and a useless loss of werewolf life.

We decided to take the fight to the alpha and his son. Markus, Theo, and David came with us. We piled into the SUV and headed out on the old dirt road that led into Northwood territory.

I was transported back to the day I'd been exiled, kicked out of my pack and the only life I'd ever known with whatever I could fit into the trunk of my car. I'd come a long way from that naive doe-eyed girl with no family or home to speak of.

I wasn't Talia Linetti, daughter of the alpha's punching bag and scapegoat, anymore. I was Talia Long Claw, Princess of the Bone Clan.

And the Northwood alpha was about to find out exactly what that meant.

# CHAPTER 15
# TALIA

We didn't bother with a sneak attack, slipping through the woods over property lines. I wanted Maddox and his father to see me coming.

"You're sure about this?" Galen tried one last time to convince me not to go through with my plan and wanted to challenge the Northwood alpha himself.

But I wanted justice, for my father, for my mother – for myself.

And I would have it.

"Galen, we've been through this." I cupped his jaw in my hand and ran the pad of my thumb along his cheek. "I know you're worried—"

"Damn right I am, and you would be too if I was the one fighting." Galen stepped back out of my reach and raked his fingers through his hair. "Talia, please. I'm begging you."

"You're not even on your knees." I teased, my tone playful, and winked at him. When his frown deepened and brows pinched together, I sighed and gave up on lightening the mood. "When you *asked* me to stay out home while you went out and fought demons, I agreed because of the risks, and I trust your judgment. I'm *asking* you to trust mine."

I put emphasis on the word asked because he hadn't. It was a gentle, if not much needed reminder that while I'd agreed to his demands it wasn't going to be a habit. We were a team and we needed to trust each other.

"How are the risks to you or the baby any different now?" Galen's eyes glimmered with a golden ring around his iris. His wolf was close to the surface but he kept him, along with his temper, in check.

"I fought him before and won." I said, reminding him of the last breech in our defenses by the Northwood pack.

"You weren't pregnant then, Talia." His crumpled expression and hand splayed across my abdomen were almost enough to change my mind.

Almost.

Besides, I wouldn't risk the Long Claw pack any more than I already had. If I lost, they still had their alpha and were protected. If Galen lost, Maddox and his father would take control of our pack, putting me and the baby in more danger than ever before.

I explained as much.

"If you lost, what do you think would happen to me and the baby?" I asked, nudging him toward the only possible conclusion. "You and I both know it's a real possibility if you challenge him because he won't fight fair. He'll find some way to cheat."

"And he won't with you?" Galen scoffed.

"I'm a woman. He doesn't think he'll have to." I covered his hand, still resting on my belly, with mine. "Trust me, I know him. If he can't beat me fair and square, he'll think it's a sign of weakness to the other members of the pack, undermining his authority and leaving himself open to another challenge. He wouldn't risk it."

"You could run." Galen clung to hope like a security blanket.

Not that I could blame him.

I used to think of myself as an optimist. Perhaps I would be again. Once we removed the Northwood alpha from power and brought the remaining pack members into the fold.

Until then my future and my baby's future were uncertain.

Maddox and his father ripped away my rose-colored glasses with my father's murder and expulsion from the pack, leaving me hopeless. But it was the subsequent events that made me a realist.

I'd been willing to risk it all to save Galen back in Alaska. Nothing had changed since we returned home.

He looked like he wanted to protest again, but I raised my hand, cutting his argument off before he started.

"Whether you fight him, or I fight him, if Northwood wins there's no future for me." I skipped the sugar coating and stripped the truth down to its barest form.

"Yeah, because that makes me feel a lot better." Galen took my hands in his, raised them to his lips and brushed a kiss against my fingertips. "Tell me you can do this. Tell me you're going to beat the alpha and win the Northwood pack."

"I can and I will." I said, with every ounce of confidence that I could muster.

It was an easy promise to make and one I intended to keep.

We drove into town and pulled right up to the alpha's front door. Galen and I got out of the SUV, with Markus, Theo, and David at our backs, climbed the porch steps and knocked on the door.

"What the hell?" Maddox opened the front door, eyes wide with shock and mistrust as he sized up our party. He narrowed his gaze when he worked his way back to me and Galen. "Dad, you are not going to believe who's at the door."

Maddox crossed his arms over his chest and leaned against the door jamb, crossing his legs at the ankles. He was every bit the arrogant asshole, having shucked the charming façade he'd used to lure me in with lies about a mating bond.

I had no idea what I'd ever seen in him.

The alpha came to the door, scanning the faces of the people on his porch and no doubt assessing us in order of who posed the greatest threat to him and his pack. I knew where he'd rank me - at the bottom.

And I was counting on it.

"Well, well, well, if it isn't Galen Long Claw. You've come to hand over your pack? Fine. I accept." The alpha scratched the stubble on his jaw as if he were contemplating a legitimate offer. "Just take the trash out with you when you leave. We sure as hell don't have a use for her."

I wasn't entirely sure what his use for me had ever been. Considering how much he hated me and my mother, I couldn't fathom why he ever permitted Maddox to date me, let alone propose.

It certainly wasn't for breeding.

He made his feelings for me and my kind loud and clear.

There was no way he would ever have allowed our bloodlines to mix. The only logical explanation had been to keep an eye one me. I'd yet to exhibit any signs of my demon wolf heritage while in the Northwood pack, but as my father-in-law he would have been able to keep a close eye on me to see if I ever did. He was right to be suspicious of that.

And if I'd been a member of his pack when the laten traits manifested he would have killed me for it.

"Asshole." Theo masked his insult in a fake cough.

Markus and David delivered elbow jabs from either side of him with mutters for him to shut up and let me handle the alpha as planned.

"My name isn't Linetti. Not anymore." I stepped forward and took the lead position in our group with the added confidence that Galen was there, lending me some of his strength through our bond. "I am Talia Long Claw, Princess of the Deofol Bone Clan. I came here to facilitate your resignation and the transition to new leadership."

"What?" Maddox shook his head, seemingly hung up on my titles.

"It's a challenge, son." The alpha clapped his hand on Maddox's shoulder with an air of confidence he hadn't earned. He laughed in my face and shook his head, a mixture of shock and disbelief in his eyes. "And am I understanding this right? Talia is the one making it?"

"Do you accept my challenge?" I held my head high and met his gaze in a simple act of defiance. "Or am I presenting it before the national council?"

He narrowed his gaze into a withering glare that, just a few weeks earlier, would have had me cowering before him. It seemed like a lifetime ago when I'd been that naïve, that weak.

But I wasn't that wolf anymore and it was time Northwood met the real me.

"I accept." The alpha pushed past his son and strolled out onto the front porch. "After you."

He kicked off his shoes and padded out to the front lawn and gave me the "come on" gesture to join him in the yard.

I'd watched the alpha fight and fought him myself before. The man had nothing on Alita. I learned more from one fight with the captain of Leto's guard than I had in any of my previous fights. Not that there were many. Women weren't given the opportunity to learn to defend themselves in the Northwood pack.

But I wasn't a Northwood wolf. Not anymore. In truth, I never was one.

I let the alpha come to me, landing counter punches whenever he threw one of his own. I kept my guard up, especially around my stomach, avoiding body blows to keep the baby safe from injury during the challenge.

I'd expected him to stay on his feet longer, that he would assume he could easily take me in my human form, but I was ready for his shift. I felt the magical charge in the air, like static electricity, just before he transformed.

And I met his wolf with mine.

She stood on all fours, a ferocious, growling, snarling white beast with red soul piercing eyes. The alpha wasn't ready for her, to come face to face with the princess of a demon wolf pack.

My red eyes threw him off and I used them to my advantage. I lunged for his throat, my incisors piercing through fur and hide, down into the muscle. Blood poured from his wounds. Bile would have rose in the back of my throat at the first hint of coppery tang on my tongue, but my wolf's taste wasn't as delicate.

The alpha growled, and snarled, twisted, and writhed, until he shook himself free of me. I hit the ground with a thud, landing on my side, and scrambled to all four as he rounded on me with lips curled back and fangs extended.

Saliva dripped from his canine teeth, and froth formed in his mouth like a rabid animal. In a way, I supposed he was. His left ear twitched and right front foot pawed the ground. He charged, jaws snapping, and slashed at my side.

"Talia." Galen shouted my name from the sidelines, unable to hide the fear in his voice.

I knew what it cost him to stand by and watch me fight the alpha on my own. He was my mate, an alpha, it was in his very nature to want to protect me – even when I didn't need or want him to. It made me love him all the more, and I empathized with his situation – because our roles could be reversed one day.

But I also knew his fear wasn't just for me, but the baby I carried – because I felt it too.

The alpha lapped at the blood on his paw and howled. Maddox answered from his perch on the porch railing, his feet hanging over the side. He cheered his father on, certain of a victory, while antagonizing Galen about leaving the future of his pack to an immature, inexperienced girl.

"She's had plenty of experience." Galen shot back, goading Maddox with the double meaning.

The reminder that not only had I learned to fight alongside my mate, but I'd also learned other things as well, had the desired effect. Maddox pushed off this railing and dropped to the ground, a small cloud of dirt pluming at his feet. He grabbed his tee shirt by the hem, yanked it over his head, and stalked toward Galen.

The alpha growled and jerked his head toward the porch, reminding his son of his place – behind him. Maddox heeded his father's warning and sat on the porch steps like a petulant prince on a broken throne.

I snarled, drawing the alpha's attention and ire back to where it belonged – on me and the challenge. I ran at him, teeth and claws barred, and swiped with my paw, slashing his jaw. My declaw hooked his lip like a fish on a line, but instead of reeling him in, I pulled hard and ripped through his mouth.

Blood ran down his jaw and throat, making him look more like a demon wolf than me. At least his outward appearance finally matched the monstrous bastard within. He charged again, feigned right and zig-zagged left at the last second. He latched onto my hind leg with his claws and raked them from tail to paw when I pulled free.

I fought the urge to whimper when I tested my weight on my back leg and hobbled around to face the alpha. Unable to attack, I adjusted my position and balanced myself on three legs instead of four and waited for the alpha to make another move.

He didn't make me wait long.

The alpha would have smelled my blood, sensed my weakness, and not wanted to give me the smallest opportunity to heal my injuries. He launched himself at me again and I braced myself for the impact.

I took the hit and rolled onto my good side, keeping our combined weight off my injured leg, hooked my dewclaw into his underside and dragged it along the soft flesh of his belly.

Warmth seeped into my skin as his blood soaked through my coarse fur.

He pinned me with his front paws and snarled, but the fight had already left him. I heard it in his voice and saw it in his eyes. Not to mention the blood loss.

I barred my teeth, reared up, clamped down onto his neck until my teeth met and his larynx was crushed.

The alpha's limp body landed in a heap when I unlocked my jaws and pushed him off me. He shifted back to his human form when the last piece of his soul left his body.

Maddox made a strangled sound. Not unlike the one I'd made the day my father had been killed. I knew his pain and wouldn't have wished on him or anyone else. But it was hard to find pity – for either of them.

If I thought his father would have let me live in peace, we wouldn't have ended up on his doorstep. But that would never have happened.

Not so long as the alpha had air in his lungs.

Maddox never made a formal challenge to avenge his father and reclaim his birthright to lead the Northwood pack. He leapt off the porch steps, shifted in mid-air and collided with my mate.

Galen, still in his human form, intercepted Maddox before he could lay one fang or claw on my body and slammed him to the ground. Galen clamped one hand around Maddox's jaws, forcing them closed. He wrapped his other arm around his neck, slipping it between his forearm and Maddox's throat, and gripped his bicep with his free hand. Galen's legs swung around Maddox's body and locked at the ankles before he arched his entire body backward, snapping his neck with an audible pop.

It was the end of an era for the Northwood pack, but a new beginning – for those that wanted it.

We gave them an honorable death and burial which was more than they'd given my father and more than they deserved.

Once we merged the packs and things had settled down, I planned to find the graves of my parents and have them relocated to the Long Claw cemetery with proper headstones and a traditional burial.

Removing the alpha was only step one. There were other likeminded wolves that needed to be exiled if we were ever to have peace between the packs and in our town.

Fortunately, weeding them out would be easy. I knew them all by name. They were the same wolves who stood behind the alpha cheering him on when he murdered my father and cast me out of the only family I'd ever known.

We had a long road ahead of us. There would be ups and downs. Disagreements. But there would also be friendships, mates, marriages. New life created and celebrated alongside our elders. Merging two large packs into one wasn't going to be an easy task, but Galen and I had proven that we were up to the challenge - and the end result would be worth it.

We'd fought for so long, over so little and it was time for

both the Northwood and Long Claw packs to put the past behind them and learn to live together.

The demon threat was gone, and so was the threat of attack from another wolf pack. We were safe, happy, and starting a family.

We were building our future. Our children's future. Our pack's future.

# CHAPTER 16

# TALIA

It had been six months of arduous work and we were far from living in a utopia, but overall, the new pack was thriving.

And so was our family.

Galen and I made what had felt like a difficult decision at the time, and had a new house built on the Long Claw property. He had so many wonderful memories in his father's house, and I had my share of happy memories with Max as well, but in the end, we found them to be clouded with the memory of how he'd been taken from us too soon.

We'd worked to give all the wolves in town a fresh start. Galen and I deserved the same.

The four-bedroom cabin had a wrap-around porch with stunning views of the property that included a little shed warded with magic on the back of our lot.

Galen wanted it torn down, the embarrassment of what he'd done still haunted him. But I made a strong argument, which may or may not have involved chaining myself to the outbuilding in protest and convinced him otherwise. That was where Galen and I first met, where our fates changed and became forever entwined. He'd seen it as a reminder of our past until I convinced him that it was really a reminder of our future.

We'd decorated the nursery in soft creams and butter yellows after deciding to wait until the baby was born to find out if we were having a boy or a girl. I'd almost caved at the last sonogram appointment and had nearly convinced Galen to go along with it. But we'd waited seven and a half months. We could wait a few weeks more. Soon enough we would be fighting over who changed the last diaper or warmed the last bottle.

I for one couldn't wait.

Neither could Galen. He was by my side every step of the way through the pregnancy, never missing an appointment with the midwife. He never complained about paint samples, assembling the crib, or midnight runs to the convenience store for another one of my crazy cravings. He was all in, hands on and was going to be an amazing father.

"How did I know you'd be in here?" Galen walked into the nursery with an arm full of soft yellow baby blankets and an oversized teddy bear.

"Because it's my happy place?" I sank my bare toes into the plush area rug and pushed against the floor with the balls of my feet, restarting the gentle rhythm of the old fashioned, wooden rocking chair.

"Mine too." Galen propped the teddy bear on top of the dresser and tucked the blankets away in the drawers. He pulled a folded slip of paper out of his back pocket and held it out to me. "The list."

We'd spent weeks whittling down the list of names. Adding, removing, adding, removing until we reached a top three for names for a son and a top three for a daughter.

"Nope. The list is complete. No more changes." I waved my hand, playfully smacking the list away. "Besides, I already told you, we'll know which one of the names suits their sweet, chubby little face when we meet them. They'll pick their own name."

"Okay, I know better to argue with you." Galen came up from behind me, eased the rocker back and leaned down placing a kiss on my forehead. "When are you going to say yes and marry me, already? Let's make it official."

"Our fated mate mark already made it official." I rested my hands over my swollen belly and closed my eyes, a smile forming when I felt a healthy kick beneath my palm.

"Talia." Galen mixed my name with a soft growl. "I'm serious."

"I know you are and that's why your reaction is so adorable." I eased myself out of the rocking chair and reached for Galen.

But he was already on bended knee, with a small black velvet box in his trembling hands. He pried open the lid, revealing a sparkling diamond fixed in a platinum setting with smaller inlaid stones that formed the shape of a star.

The same start that was in our fated mate mark.

"Talia, please make me the luckiest wolf in the world and say that you'll marry me." He pulled the ring from its box, took my left hand in his, but waited for me to say the words before slipping it on my ring finger.

"Of course, I'll marry you."

With our baby due within the month, we didn't have time for an elaborate ceremony once I accepted Galen's proposal. Which was more than fine as far as I was concerned. Standing on ceremony was never really our style. Galen and I had had an unconventional romance. Our wedding was the same way. We fell hard, fast and fought like hell to be together. Our union wasn't about the dress or a huge guest list. It was about our love for each other.

Under a full moon and a sky full of stars we stood before our friends, packmates and took our vows to love, and cherish each other.

I'd chosen a simple cream wedding dress from a bridal shop in town that had lace bell sleeves and pearl beading at the empire waist. The gown highlighted my swollen belly and I'd never felt more beautiful. In place of a tiara or veil I wore a hand-woven crown of wildflowers from Sarah's garden pinned into the nest of golden curls piled on top of my head.

She'd returned home along with the rest of the coven members. If I hadn't known they'd stayed on pack land, I wouldn't have guessed by looking at the property. There was no evidence of their encampment left behind. The witches, under Marguerite's guidance had performed a spell that restored the land down to the last blade of grass.

I'd missed Sarah living so close and was glad to have her by my side on such a joyous occasion. We became fast friends under unusual circumstances. She was a confidant, the first person I'd shared my demon wolf side with and was the closest thing to a sister I had.

"Stop crying. You'll ruin your makeup." Sarah placed one final pin the floral crown on top of my head. She pecked my on the cheek, grabbed the handkerchief of the bathroom vanity and dabbed my eyes.

"It's waterproof mascara." I smiled, gave a soft chuckle, and took the ivory linen trimmed in lace from her, careful not to get any smudges of color on it. "Thank you for being my maid of honor. I'm so happy you're here."

"The honor is mine, Mrs. Long Claw." Sarah smiled and fussed with the curls she'd set inside the circle of flowers on my head. She stepped back, eyed her work, and approved of her masterpiece with one last spritz of hairspray. "There, perfect. You are stunning."

"I'm not Mrs. Long Claw, yet." I reminded her, pushing out the small stool from under the bathroom counter and standing on my feet.

I'd opted to go barefoot. Shoes became uncomfortable late into my pregnancy and the sound of flipflops announcing my presence as I walked down the aisle was not how I wanted to make my entrance. With the weather warm, and the wedding outside, shoes were not required.

Besides, I loved the feel of soft grass beneath my feet. Sarah painted my toes a delicate shade of neutral pink after I'd given up the effort. It felt like a long time since I'd seen them properly.

Despite the aches and pains of the last days of the last term, I wanted to be a mother more than anything else and I was beyond happy that Galen convinced me to marry him – for real.

Not that I ever planned on telling him that.

"Well, we better get you down to your groom so you can be." Sarah gave my shoulders a quick squeeze, looped her arm through mine and led me carefully down the stairs.

I hitched the hem of my dress as I descended the stairs and followed behind her through the house out to the backyard where Galen waited for me.

He watched with a watery gaze as I made my way down the grassy aisle to meet him beneath the old living oak in the center of the pack lands where the monthly full moon festivities were held.

This full moon festival proved to be unlike any other.

Marguerite performed the ceremony. She'd met with Galen and I a week before our big day to help each of us write our vows. Mine were more of an outline, something to guide me as I stood before our family and friends and spoke from my heart with promises to love Galen until the end of my days.

I waited on pins and needles to hear him speak the words he'd written for me.

Nyssa, Celia and Sarah had walked ahead of me and lined the aisle on my left. Markus, Theo and David stood with Galen on my right. Long Claw and Northwood wolves filled the metal folding chairs that had been set out in rows across the field.

Picnic tables loaded with homemade dishes like salads, grilled meats, pastries and pies. A three tiered chocolate cake with cream cheese buttercream icing, decorated with the same wildflowers that adorned my head, stood in the center of the country style buffet.

The sight and sweet smell of the sugary confection made

my mouth water, but nothing like the man in the off-white seersucker suit waiting for me at the end of the aisle.

After everything we'd been through separately and together, we deserved our happily ever after.

A home, a healthy pack, and a family

Galen and I opted to skip the honeymoon. We both felt we'd done enough traveling as of late and there wasn't any place that we wanted to be other than the home we'd made for ourselves. The midwife had also advised against any trips so late in the pregnancy.

We were one step closer to having everything we'd ever dreamed of. The only thing left to do for our happy ending to be complete was to welcome home our first little bundle of joy.

Less than a week after the wedding, the first labor pain let me know that our baby was well on their way. Galen rushed around the house, grabbing towels, hot water and the rest of the supplies for a home birth on the list that the midwife provided. He was a nervous wreck, but coached my breathing, held my hand and stayed by my side throughout the labor and delivery.

Eight hours later under a waning moon, Luna Lowella Long Claw was born.

"She's the most beautiful thing I've ever seen." Galen cradled our daughter in his arms. "We did this. We made this amazing little creature. You and me, Talia."

Luna stole her father's heart right out from under me and wrapped him around his little finger the moment she opened those big, bright eyes and looked at him. I knew how he felt. I hadn't thought it possible to love anyone more than my husband until I met my daughter.

She was perfect in every way, with fair hair, sapphire eyes, chubby cheeks, and ten tiny fingers and toes. Even her little cries were music to my ears.

Luna was a moon wolf, it was in her name and in her blood, and had the world at her feet. Our daughter was small, but she was fierce. I felt it through the special bond that only a mother and child shared. I couldn't wait to watch her grow up and see what would become of our little alpha.

When Galen plucked me off the street, I never expected to be so happy. After the losses I'd suffered I hadn't thought it possible. He'd found me at my lowest and helped me pick up the pieces of my tattered life. I planned to spend the rest of my life showering him with my love and gratitude.

He was my lover, my best friend.

My fated mate.

Thank you for reading the sixth and final book in the Shifter
Rejected series. I hope you enjoyed reading it as much as I loved
writing it.

If you're keen to start another series of mine, I would definitely
recommend "The Stolen Fae." It is a little steamier, but is a
beautiful romance.

The link to download FREE book 1 is:
https://books2read.com/stolenfae

Otherwise, read on for a sneak peek into book 1:

# CHAPTER 1

# AURELIA

I sprinted through the city center and passed the wards into the witch market. My kind weren't welcome in this part of Dallas, but I had little choice in the matter.

I pulled my hood lower over my face and did my best to keep away from the other patrons. The apothecary was my target, so as I approached the shop I hurried to the door, then scurried inside. The woman who owned the shop ignored me until I walked up to the counter with my purchase.

"You don't belong here, girl." The woman sneered. "I only serve witches, not filthy beasts like you."

"I need this for my mother," I said firmly, pushing the purchase across the glass counter.

She knew exactly who my adoptive mother was and wouldn't question the fact I was here to buy something for her. But the shop owner loved to look down upon me, and hassled me anytime I came in on behalf of the woman who'd taken me in.

*It's the same song and dance every time.*

"One of these days you won't have her to hide behind, mutt," she grumbled but rang up my purchase all the same.

Anger rose in gut, making my fingers tighten into fists and my jaw clench tight.

*I'm not a shifter,* I wanted to scream but it was easier for everyone to think that.

The alternative was too dangerous for me.

My wings fluttered at my back, thankfully still glamoured from prying eyes.

I took the bag the woman thrust back at me, then shuffled from the shop.

*I need to get home.*

I wove through the crowd careful to keep my wings from brushing any unsuspecting witches or shifters.

"Watch it," I said as a man bumped into my back and I shivered at the strange pain that came with the move.

*Shit, my wings are sensitive today.*

"Well, hello there, pretty. I didn't see you there." The man turned to stare at me with a sinister smile and sniffed the air around me. He was trying to work out what I was, and I couldn't have that. Not today. Not any day.

I bowed my head and skirted around him, cursing my temper. I should have just kept moving. But the man's hand latched around my arm in a bruising grip, stopping me from going any further.

"I don't want any trouble," I ground out between my teeth.

His eyes trailed over me as he pulled my hood down. "What are you?" He pulled me closer to him.

"I'm none of your concern," I spat and wrenched my arm from his grip.

"I think you are." He reached for me again, but I raced away before he could catch me.

Shouts followed me as I pushed through other patrons to escape.

*Does he know what I am? How the hell could he smell me like that?*

"That shifter girl stole from me," The man bellowed from behind me. "Stop her."

*Shit, shit, shit.*

I rushed through the market but the man had caused a stir and more witches pointed at me to aid in my capture.

"I didn't steal anything, he's crazy," I shouted as I passed several women who glared at me and then started screaming to help the man capture me.

"Freaking witches," I grumbled under my breath ducking into an alley.

Several men in black uniforms ran past the opening to the alley as I hid behind a large garbage skip. The scent of rotting garbage made me retch.

*Gods, that's disgusting.*

I gripped the bag that I got from the apothecary as I stepped out from behind the dumpster and scanned the area for the closest threat.

*How the fuck do I get out of this mess?*

The man who started the chase stepped into the mouth of the alley and grinned at me.

"You really are a pretty one and you will make me some good money." His eyes twinkled as he stepped closer.

"I'm not going to make you anything," I growled at him as I scanned the alley for a possible escape.

There was a fence behind me leading to an alley.

*Can I fly over the fence without being seen? He obviously already knows what I am but what's on the other side? Will humans see me? I can't risk it. Can I?*

Something flashed in the man's hand and my eyes widened at the silver weapon.

*Is that a gun? Is he going to shoot me with iron?*

I shuddered. "Are you going to shoot me?" I asked with a raised brow.

Being pumped full of iron was not my idea of fun.

"This thing?" he asked flashing me a grin as he waved his gun around. "It won't kill you; it will just make you sleepy so I can get you where we're going."

"I'm not going anywhere with you." I sneered and unfurled my wings. He couldn't see them but it made me feel better to know I could act.

*I need to get home.*

My mother was waiting for the medicine that I'd bought. I needed to get it to her before it was too late.

"Oh, but you don't have a choice. Do you know what will happen if the other witches see your wings?" He asked with a grin.

My stomach fell as I pulled my wings back to my body.

*He knows what I am and what the witches will do if they figure it out. Shit.*

"You can threaten me all you want. I can take care of myself," I said and crossed my arms over my chest.

"What if I'm not threatening you?" He asked with a raised brow. "What if I'm promising you a better life?"

I laughed at his words and pointed to the metal object in his hand.

"That looks like enough of a threat to me. I don't need your help or a better life. I'm perfectly fine where I am."

He raised the gun with a frown. I knew he had no intention of letting me go.

I unfurled my wings behind me. My freedom was more important than wherever he thought I would have a better life.

*Even if I'm outed to the witches it's still better than whatever plans this mercenary has for me.*

I crouched down ready to jump in the air. My wings weren't used to flying since I had been banned from doing so my whole life, but I would use whatever advantage I had to get away from the tranquilizer gun that was pointed at my heart.

"Stop," he shouted and cocked the gun. "I would rather take you in willingly. There are things you should know."

"Bullshit," I said shaking my head. "There's nothing you can tell me that I don't already know."

"Really?" He chuckled. "I would have to disagree on that. My employer would very much like to tell you the truth about who and what you are."

I burst into a fit of laughter as I bounced on the balls of my feet and jumped into the air.

"Stop," the man shouted and a soft click sounded when he pulled the trigger.

I soared up above the chain link fence behind me and even

higher when a pinch to my shoulder made me flinch. An iron bullet.

*Shit. It got me.*

I landed on the concrete at the other end of the alley and stumbled. My head was spinning as I leaned against the wall.

*Don't stop. You have to keep going. He knows where you are.* The mental pep talk barely helped as I shook away the fog from my brain.

I took a few stumbling steps before getting my bearings and remembering where I was. I was still inside the wards and only a couple of blocks away from home.

*I can do this.*

I pulled my hood over my head and strolled out into the bustling crowd attempting to get lost in the shuffle. I couldn't afford for the man to catch up to me again. He couldn't find me.

I needed to get home with the medicine for my mother.

It only took about fifteen minutes before I saw the little Italian restaurant our apartment sat above and I swayed on my feet as I rounded the corner to the alley where the fire escape sat.

I crawled up the ladder barely able to hold my eyes open. My eyes blinking groggily as the poison from the lead coursed through me.

*How am I going to give mother her medicine when I can barely keep my eyes open?*

I made it to the balcony outside our downtown apartment and crawled to the window.

My arms were as weak as jelly as I lifted the window and rolled inside the living room. The plush carpet broke my fall and I groaned and pushed to my knees. I held my head in my hands as I blinked my eyes to clear the black spots in my vision.

*Just a little while longer. I need to get the tincture to her.*

I crawled across the beige carpet of the living room, not even noticing the cream walls. My sole focus was on the door at the end of the hall.

My arms shook and I slumped to the floor just outside my mother's door.

*I'm so tired. I need to sleep.*

My vision swirled again as I battled past the fatigue and reached for the handle, but came up short as my eyes closed again.

A muffled moan woke me up, and my eyes shot open.

*How long have I been asleep and why am I on the floor in the hallway?*

My brain was fuzzy as my gaze hit the cream colored door of my mother's bedroom and my fist tightened, crinkling the small plastic bag in my hand.

*The tincture. Shit. Is mother, okay?*

Another muffled moan sounded, and I winced, pulling myself to standing.

"Mother?" I called through the door as I cracked it open.

The room was dark, just as I left it and my mother's still form was on the bed.

I took two large steps in her direction holding out the medicine for her but stopped short.

*How long was I out from that tranquilizer? Is she okay?*

Mother's chest didn't rise and fall like it should and pain lanced through my chest.

*No, she can't be gone. She's the only person I have in the world.*

Tears blurred my vision as I sat heavily at the edge of her bed. She hadn't been a great mother to me. I'd been little more than a slave to her, but she had shielded me from those who would have wanted me dead or for even more nefarious purposes.

*Like that man in the market.*

I hunched over her body, her skin cold to the touch and whispered the words of the witches last rites. I hated that she was gone and that it was my fault for getting caught by that man in the market.

*If I ever see him again, I will kill him where he stands.*

My mother wouldn't have wanted me to waste time. She would have wanted me to run from those who would suspect foul play in her death.

She'd often told me that if something happened to her, I needed to run far and fast. Even as the tears coursed down my cheeks, I resolved what I would do.

Mother had not given birth to me. She had found me and saved me. Given me a roof over my head. Food. Clothing.

Now, I refused to be caught and killed or used. I would finally be free because that is what she had wanted for me.

I wiped a tear from my eye as I whispered one last prayer hoping it would take her into the afterlife before turning and leaving the room. I didn't know where I was going or how I would survive but I would.

But I would do it for her, the one person who ever cared that I would be more than I was perceived to be, or I would die trying.

Jumping to my feet, I marched into the small room that I called my own. It wasn't really a bedroom, more of a closet with blankets and some clothes stacked on the floor but it had been mine. I packed a bag and got ready to leave when someone pounded on the front door.

Bang. Bang. Bang.

*Shit. Did someone see me? Are they here to take me away?*

My head swiveled and I looked between the front door and my bedroom window, indecision warring within me. My own self-preservation won out just as mother would have wanted. I opened the window climbing down the fire escape toward freedom.

I had no place to go and no clue what I was going to do, but I had to run for my life and hope I could figure it all out along the way.

~

Download for FREE now:
https://books2read.com/stolenfae